The Unwanted Guest and Other Short Thrillers

Timothy R. Baldwin

Published by Indies United Publishing House, LLC, 2024.

Copyright © 2024 Timothy R. Baldwin

www.timothyrbaldwin.com

First Edition published March 2024

By Indies United Publishing House, LLC

Cover design by Reb Claudio https://www.fiverr.com/lanrebclaudio

Story art by Maggie Malia

ISBN: 978-1-64456-704-3 (paperback)

ISBN: 978-1-64456-705-0(ePub)

Library of Congress Control Number: 2024901423

INDIES UNITED PUBLISHING HOUSE, LLC
P.O. BOX 5071
QUINCY, IL 62305-5071

www.indiesunited.net

Table of Contents

For those who desire to read, but have very little time. Believe me, I know the feeling.

No Signal

MY eyes flutter open as daylight pours into my room. It takes me a moment to get my bearings. When I do, I curse and hop out of bed. I grab a wad of clothing. Slacks and a dress shirt, both wrinkled, would have to do.

I glance at my phone.

7:58 am.

Even in my haste to throw on whatever, I will be late. Meanwhile, my students will already be in homeroom.

I grab my phone and thumb through the device. Something went wrong last night.

I freeze.

Not a single alarm exists on my phone. This, despite having the phone for some six months.

"Jeanne, did you —"

The bathroom door creaks.

Venturing into the bathroom, I am immediately bombarded with the pungent smell of sewage. I turn on the faucet. Air sputters through the valves until a splash of dark brown water pours into the tub.

Jeanne, I conclude, probably discovered the same thing this morning and ditched me to go to her place. Was I such a letdown last night that she didn't even bother to wake me?

For now, I opt to call into work. As the phone rings, I wrack my brain. There had to be a logical explanation for the phone and the apparent backup in the bathroom.

On the second ring, the school secretary answers the phone.

"It's a great day at Chesterton High School," she begins cheerfully. "How can I help you?"

"Hey, Linda. This is Alek. I was calling to —"

"Alek? What's your last name?"

"Petrov."

She shuffles through what sounds like papers. "Mr. Petrov?"

"Yes?"

"Are you late for an IEP meeting for your child?"

"No. I work there."

"What do you teach?"

"Are you kidding?" I ask. "Science. You filed my paperwork when the school first hired me last summer."

"I'm sorry—"

"I've been working there for over a year!"

"Sir. You're going to have to calm down. I'm sorry. I've never seen your paperwork or name come across my desk."

"Linda, I'm not sure what's going on, but —"

"Maybe you have the wrong number?"

I exhale as I grit my teeth. "Maybe. I'll try another number."

I sit on the edge of my bed and stare at a gaping hole in the wall. Jeanne and I must've had a wild night. Only I can't remember any of it.

I do a mental walk-through of last night's events. A group of teachers from Chesterton High met up at the pub. At the end of the bar, a stunning woman eyed me with a sly smile. Josh, one of my coworkers, nudged me. My drink spilled. The woman laughed, then called the bartender over. As she ordered, she nodded toward me.

The bartender handed me a shot. "The lady would like to share a drink with you."

Josh nudged me off the barstool. I grabbed the drink, and my legs seemed to work of their own accord, drawing me to her.

"Sir?" A woman's voice takes me out of the moment.

The back of my throat itches. Swallowing, I lift the phone to my ear. "Yes? I'm here."

The woman chuckles. "Oh, good. I thought I lost you there, Mr. Petrov. Did you get the number?"

My eyes wander back to the hole in the wall. "Thanks for your help."

"Have a —"

I end the call.

My thoughts go back to Jeanne as I rub my temples. I try to recall something vivid about her. Her eyes had been captivating. Yet, even these remain an abstraction, as though my mind's eye has gone completely blind.

I tap the phone's screen and find the email app. The inbox is empty. More to the point, no accounts are set up. Like my alarms, it's as if my digital life has been erased. But did they account for my knowing the username and passwords of all my accounts?

I grin. I'll shoot an email to Josh. He could fill in the details of last night's escapades. I select the option to enter a new account. Like my inability to visualize the woman, the account information hovers in a blurry haze on my memory's periphery.

I sense this has happened before, not to me, per se, but to those who wish for a reboot.

Blank faces and blank papers flash in my memory as I lecture incoherently about something important. Details escape me, and I am left with the emptiness one feels years after losing a pet or loved one.

This idea of loss is the most concrete thing I've been able to recall all morning. After looking at my phone, I see the last number I dialed has been saved. I open a browser and conduct a search for the number. Soon, a link to Chesterton High School's website pops up.

I call the number, and a woman's familiar and cheery voice answers on the second ring.

"Hi," I say. "This is Alek —"

"Hi, Mr. Petrov!"

My heart flutters. *Is that recognition in Linda's voice?*

"Did you figure things out?" she adds before I can respond.

Recognition. Yes. But not because the woman knows me.

I hang up.

Another idea comes to my mind. I've kept paper records of every bank statement I've ever gathered. Even my birth certificate and passport are all locked safely away in a —

My eyes drift to the hole in the wall. I swallow a burning lump in my throat, and it travels with acidic foreboding to the pit of my stomach. Whatever happened occurred last night. Someone, probably the woman I brought home, drugged me. Then, they found my place of employment and my accounts and systematically eradicated my existence in some sick social experiment.

I needed to move. Whoever did this couldn't be too far ahead of me.

I launch my phone and watch with satisfaction as it shatters to pieces. Then I sift through the remains and find the SIM card. This, too, I destroy, making it that much more difficult for anyone to track me.

I enter the hallway and make my way downstairs. My nostrils flare as I breathe in thick, moldy air.

The living room walls are bare. Clear plastic layered with dust covers furniture that isn't mine. I flip the switch, but the lights don't work. I go to the kitchen, and my stomach growls at the sight of the refrigerator. When I open it, I gag. Nothing but rot and mold. I slam the door shut.

———⊬⊬⟍⟍⟍⊬⊬———

NONE OF THIS MAKES sense. This is my house. Almost every part of it is familiar, but the paint is faded and peeling. It seems no one, including myself, has lived in this house for years.

But wasn't it just last night that I came home from a bar? With a woman, even? I'd like to say we had a good time, but I can't remember. It's as if I exist in a time warp where past and present overlap. Still, a subtle memory tugs at the corner of my mind, just out of reach with hues of blues and reds.

Dance music begins with a steady drumbeat. Patrons, Josh, and my coworkers begin gyrating on the dance floor. The woman, Jeanne, leans into me. She smells of sweat and vanilla.

"Hey," she says. "Wanna dance?"

I down my drink. "Let's go."

I take her hand, and lights flash around me. Shading my eyes, I turn to her.

She's gone.

A glare catches on the front blinds of the house. I rush to the window and disrupt a layer of dust as I yank on the drawstring. The blinds crash to the floor, and I jump away. Through the haze of the window, I spot my car. Rust speckles its faded blue paint. The driveway pavement is caked with crabgrass, and seedlings have taken root in several large cracks. The rest of the neighborhood is old—maybe by thirty years.

Vacant houses with caved-in roofs seem to frown at me. My house is the only one with a car in the driveway.

The air inside the living room swelters and drives me outside, where the air carries the scent of fire. As I glance from one end of the street to the other, I am flooded with images of a past I never experienced. An ancient explosion rocks the house, and glass shatters from within. Strange that this would be the first vivid memory to divide a blank canvas incapable of nothing more than the idea of a thing.

A scream breaks the silence of the neighborhood. I turn in time to see a figure of a woman running away from me. She glances back, and I catch her profile.

Jeanne!

Her dark hair swishes as she returns to avoiding obstacles that line the streets. She leaps over a downed electrical pole and plods on.

"Wait!" I call out.

She keeps running until she vanishes like a desert mirage.

"Jeanne!"

Abandoned houses mock me as they echo back my cry of desperation. I don't bother to call out again but run, leaping over the downed electrical pole toward Jeanne's vanishing point. Plodding on, I ignore the sting of brush and branches whipping against my arms and face. Beneath me, my feet continue to pound against the concrete.

When the path thins, a massive, spoked wheel silhouetted by the sun's glare looms before me. I squint and take care to traverse the loose concrete beneath me. A large pavilion to my left houses rusted-out bumper cars beneath a dilapidated roof. To my right, a four-wheeled cart with faded red and off-white stripes leans on one broken wheel. Weeds and shattered glass seem to overtake the cart.

"Do you like what you see?" A female voice whispers with the breeze, and I spin at the sound of metallic creaking.

My sudden movement sends the pounding of a late-night hangover to my forehead. I blink back tears in my struggle to see even the phantom of life.

"Jeanne!" I call out. "Where are you?"

Her figure, beautiful and radiant, flashes. She is sitting in a bumper car, beckoning me with a pat on the seat beside her. Then she's gone. Music to my right fires off a rapid tempo, up and down, and the ground beneath me rumbles to the sound of a ride gearing up.

A red warning light flashes as a gate lowers. Sitting in a driver's seat, I stew in the idea of waiting.

Beside me, Jeanne gives me a faraway look and speaks with sensual pleasure. "Do you want to go for a ride?" She reaches her hand out to my face. "No, you wouldn't last."

A train passes, and each car is graffitied with the characters of a language I recognize but don't understand. Gradually and simultaneously, the train rusts until it screeches to a halt. Something brushes against my face, tickling my cheek. A breeze passes over me, and the thing flutters away. Somewhere beyond my reach, it has gotten caught and now flaps in the wind.

The pain in my frontal lobe travels to the back of my head, flooding my body until I realize I am lying face-up on the ground. I open my eyes and see the sun has traveled beyond high noon. With a groan, I sit up.

"Do *you* want to go for a ride?" Her question is more persistent this time.

I look up at the Ferris wheel. Ghostly memories play tricks on me. Couples in love laugh and swing on the top of the wheel, consumed in a white-hot blaze. Memory overlays memory of a past I'm damned sure I've never experienced.

But, unlike the carnival, filled with forgotten experiences, I seem to have ceased to exist in the world. Or perhaps the world as I knew it has ceased to exist. I look at my hands. They are still young and smooth. The idea of passing out papers comes to me, as does the idea of caressing a woman's naked, soft curves.

In my sudden sense of loss, I rise and turn my attention to a piece of paper flapping beneath a shard of glass. It tugs with lifelike familiarity, flashing words and images.

The ground crackles beneath my feet. Around me, the air begins to buzz, rising and falling in crescendo as a siren blares. I step on the corner of the pamphlet and kick away the shard of glass.

Flipping over the pamphlet as I pick it up, I cannot help but smile. It is an invitation to the amusement park. A Ferris wheel, tall and proud amongst much smaller attractions, incites images of a wife and children. She holds a stick of cotton candy as the children pull off one greedy bite after another. All at once, my mouth salivates as the air carries with it the salty sweetness of carnival treats.

Just as suddenly, smokey and charred ash fills my mouth and lungs. An explosion rocks the earth, sending me back to the ground. Around me, silhouettes of mothers clutching babies run through falling debris, their cries drowned out by the cacophony around us.

Tears flood my eyes and stream down my cheeks. My heart races, and I collapse to the ground. Around me, the beeping grows louder, steadily increasing as if in time with my heartbeat. I struggle to breathe as my body convulses.

"We're losing him," a woman shouts. "Someone get the defibrillator."

"It may be too late for that," a man's cold and emotionless voice says.

My eyes flutter in my struggle to awaken from this nightmare. I gasp.

"Alek," the woman's voice echoes.

"Jeanne?" I groan.

Her voice is far away. "Hook me up. I'm going in."

"You can't!" The man shouts. Urgency has replaced his lack of emotion. "Jeanne! Get back here. The system is already overloaded."

"This was my experiment," she says. "Mine! You hear me?"

"I said —"

White space interrupts him. I'm weightless in an all too familiar blank canvas. Soon, it's rebuilding itself in pixelated pieces. Blurred bodies twirl around me, and my hand grips a shot glass filled with brown liquid, vibrating in time to the music around me.

"Alek?" a woman's voice says.

I take in Jeanne's dark, striking eyes. They narrow with concern.

"What?" I say with hesitation. "Where was I?"

Jeanne looks away. "Shit!"

I toss the shot glass to the side, not caring when a bar patron curses me. I grab Jeanne's shoulders and force her to look at me.

"What the fuck happened?"

Her face pixelates and blurs with static. "I'm sorry," her voice glitches. She turns, calling to an invisible companion. "We're losing him again."

She and the bar flicker out, suddenly replaced by the graffiti I'd seen on the train cars. I grasp the outer limits of my education and recognize the series of ones and zeros. I study their patterns as they flash around me, moving more rapidly than any human eye can read. I lock onto a shutdown code. I force my will upon it, rewriting it faster than it can execute.

Soon, I regain my sight and find myself staring at Jeanne as she taps rapidly at a keyboard. She wears a white lab coat, and her thick black hair is tied up in a bun.

"Jeanne?" I ask, but my voice sounds wrong and metallic.

She looks up. A nervous smile plays at the corner of her lips. "Alek, you're back."

"Back?" I ask. I raise an arm and catch a glimpse of a steel skeletal structure. "Where's my body?"

"We have synthetic skin to cover that," Jeanne says quickly. "And we can make adjustments to your voice."

I grit what I take to be my teeth. "I don't want this."

"With some rehabilitation," she says. "You'll be fine."

"No!" I shout. Rising, I approach her. "Where's my real body?"

Jeanne backs away, blabbing something about a blast no organic body could withstand.

"He's going to self-destruct," a man shouts.

That, I realize, is the sanest thing I've experienced in recent memory. The command is easy to find within my database, and I begin the countdown.

Ten...

Nine...

"Please, Alek," Jeanne says.

Seven...

"Get out of there," a man shouts.

Five...

She yanks a drive out of the computer and takes off through a steel door.

Two...

The door bolts with a resounding thud behind her. Then, the explosion.

A red light blinks three times, and I whir to life. A message flashes across my console: *Alright, Alek, we're trying this again. This time, I promise we won't lose the signal.*

The red light blinks once, and I type back: *No signal. The experiment has failed.*

Ark to Ashes

Chet Davis

Chihuahuan Desert, Arizona

The lights flickered to the rhythm of metal-on-metal clanging above where I crouched in an access tunnel. Overhead, hidden in the ductwork, I had stashed away items in case of an emergency. I didn't trust the system we all relied upon, with good reason — I knew it intimately. More clanging came, and I ticked off the last set of dashes and dots and closed my notebook. It was not time to emerge. Not yet anyway.

Those who had made it underground still mourned the loss of those millions who wouldn't. I thank God for our survival, and now the fate of humanity rests with us. The food supply wasn't enough to sustain more than the few hundred souls who had made it below. I doubted the Surface Dwellers who survived the Great Eruption above fared much better.

The survivors below were my responsibility; I needed to protect them from the violence brooding underground, threatening to explode at any moment.

Every day, some scuffles caught the attention of Governor Ortiz, the leader of this underground ark. An otherwise peaceful community might soon become an inescapable city prison where every person fended for their own. Ortiz spoke of a police state in his last briefing, but for now, we must maintain the status quo: monitor access points, maintain the HVAC and water treatment systems, and ration food supplies.

My radio crackled. "Davis, we've got some unusual readings in Zone Five, the mechanical room."

I doubted they needed me. Still, I had to see for myself.

"I'm on my way."

I climbed through the access panel beneath me and reached up to shut and lock the door. Another few steps down the ladder and from the catwalk in Zone One, I glanced up at the access door. The clanging had stopped for now. This time tomorrow, it will likely pick up again. I imagined some poor sap trudging through several inches of volcanic ash to pound out a message to an unknown recipient. The pounding had begun during one of my shifts and continued regularly after that. I doubted this was a coincidental correspondence. Instead, someone outside knew of my existence and expected me to keep their communications secret. While the other bunkers reported improved air quality and new plant growth, this one-way correspondence via morse code reported far more bleak news.

The government, now stationed on the coastal perimeters where they received only a dusting of ash, intended to keep people underground for as long as possible. Its agencies insisted humanity's survival depended on all nine bunkers, with Bunker Nine as the focal point.

The construction of these nine bunkers had been extensive and costly. Not all involved in the development had opted to squirrel themselves underground. We needed a sustainable network of proverbial doves to seek out inhabitable land beyond the scorched earth above us. Reports came in daily from the other eight bunkers from East to West throughout the United States. For those regions that survived, volcanic ash and air toxicity still made much of the US uninhabitable. With this constant knowledge, the people of Bunker Nine accepted their fate: safety and security with the promise of a better tomorrow for their children.

I wondered if they would be so willing if they knew the truth. Six months ago, Bunker Nine's true purpose progressively revealed itself when the knocking began. Phase One would begin, though I didn't know what that would entail. I waited for the signal.

My footsteps echoed on the catwalk as I passed through a corridor leading to Zone Two. I nodded to Gary, one of the uniformed guards on patrol during my shift.

Gary nodded back. "How're things in the mechanical room?"

"Everything is copacetic," I told him.

"Have the pipes been fixed?"

His question referred to the banging on the surface. Until now, I'd convinced Gary the noise was due to knocking pipes.

"It's not an issue," I said, repeating this exchange almost verbatim from previous days. "Besides, it only happens at night when the surface is likely cooling."

Gary nodded. "I had a thought, though. What if there were survivors? What if they found our bunker and tried to get in?"

I waved him off. "You know better than to listen to the rumors and bedtime stories trending throughout the city."

Gary chuckled. "You're right. Surface Dwellers. Poor S.O.B.S. They should've prepared as we did."

Ignoring his comment, I hurried on. He didn't have a clue. No one could have truly prepared for that day.

Heck! Gary, I, and most of us below ground couldn't have prepared. Not on our own, anyway. We needed to work with the government and the corporations that funded this extensive project.

As a steamfitter and a damn good one, like everyone else below ground, I was employed by the right people. I oversaw the construction of the entire HVAC system in this underground ark. No one else knew their way around the maze of pipes and wires that cooled and heated everything and everybody, ensuring our continued survival. Fortunately, I had been able to take my family below just before devastation hit. Limited space didn't allow for extended family members and telling them about the bunker would have risked humanity's continued survival.

Still, we could've reduced the deaths. With more time and resources, we could have saved everyone. People could have even prepared on their own. But the eruption came upon us quicker than expected. And just as suddenly, we quietly herded underground.

We'd built this bunker beneath the Chihuahuan Desert in Arizona, well over one thousand miles south of Yellowstone. Even at this distance, the layers of ash and the toxicity of the air made the surface uninhabitable. The survivors banged daily on the reinforced steel in Zone One. Some chalked the daily banging up to desperation, but the rhythmic nature of the knocking and its timing implied a code. I knew of no other inside man or woman within the bunker. As far as I knew, I worked alone.

Rumors about a coup spread throughout the bunker. Governor Ortiz responded by forming a quasi-task force, but most — including Ortiz — believed a coup unlikely. Finding no new information and being unable to corroborate a single rumor, the task force quickly dissolved. But without doubt, someone with enough tenacity and explosives would be able to break through our little fortress. The survivors hadn't found the other access points, and they wouldn't be able to tap into our air and water supply. The atmosphere and water would recycle in this self-contained, self-sustaining bunker for the next hundred years. We'd likely run out of food before the recycling systems, and CO_2 scrubbers failed.

The bunker contained three levels and five zones. Zones Three through Five held residential housing, with apartments no larger than three hundred and twenty square feet. A family of four had enough room to sleep comfortably in two separate bedrooms but not enough room to spend every waking hour together. My family lived in Zone Four, just above the commissary, the mess hall, and the recreation facility. Zone One housed operations, communications, and command, while Zone Two housed the main facilities and operations. Each zone had its own mechanical rooms, which communicated with operations.

With lights out for the night, the bunker resonated with a gentle, mechanical hum. I nodded as I passed each guard patrolling the zones in upper-level catwalks. Wiith brief longing, I passed above the apartment where my wife, teenage daughter, and son slept soundly for the night. My wife and I had caught our daughter and son once or twice sneaking out for some shenanigans with a handful of other teens, but a mandatory curfew in response to lingering fears of a coup squelched any further attempts at sneaking out.

At the catwalk access door leading to Zone Five, I spun the wheel, and the door opened with a hiss. The temperature in Zone Five was noticeably warmer. Yet, a cool draft passed through the garage-sized opening between Zone Four and Five, thus maintaining a steady circulation of air, which Zone Five didn't reciprocate.

I hit the call button on the radio strapped to my shoulder. "Davis to Operations. What are the temperature readings in Zone Five?"

"Seventy-Eight."

Not alarming, but higher than the preferred seventy-two. "Is it holding?"

"It's been rising one degree every hour. Jacobs and Matthews are working on it in the mechanical room."

"Jacobs and Matthews?" I asked. "They're not on the schedule for tonight."

"They volunteered for overtime."

Those guys never volunteered for anything. They were up to something. I picked up the pace and passed over more residential apartments. Beads of sweat formed on my brow: the temperature had to be well over eighty.

Like Zone One, this mechanical room was located on the farthest side of Zone Five and well away from the residences. Any problems with the HVAC would immediately impact the closest residents. By now, their apartments had to be sweatboxes.

As if to confirm my suspicions, an apartment door opened below me.

A woman spoke. "Is that better?"

A muffled voice answered, and the woman shuffled around for a moment before retreating into her apartment. The door remained open.

I continued until I came to the access door to Zone Five's mechanical room, where I reached for the handle and recoiled from the heat.

I radioed operations. "Operations. Code Red. We've got a fire in Zone Five."

Sirens sounded, and red lights flashed. They knew the drill. They needed a quick evacuation to the neighboring zone. I didn't have much time before the seal would close over Zone Five.

I turned and raced down the catwalk toward Zone Four. The computerized countdown to total lockdown had already sounded over the speakers, and people had begun the evacuation.

Thirty-eight seconds.

Support beams started to buckle.

Thirty seconds.

The mechanical room door blew off its hinges, sending heat roaring toward my backside.

Eighteen seconds.

The bunker groaned and screamed.

Ten seconds.

Gears activated. Who else faced incineration once we were locked inside?

Two seconds.

I dove through the closing access door as flames leaped toward the remaining gap in the door. The door slammed with a resounding thud and bolted tight.

Panicked voices called out for loved ones. Residents of Zone Four joined in the search and rescue. It wouldn't take long for the rest of the bunker's residences to understand there had been a fire. Security was already on its way to assist in relocation.

My radio crackled. "Davis. Report to Bunker Command."

As the overseer of the HVAC project, I would be the subject of scrutiny. I grasped for a plausible explanation as I headed to Bunker Command.

A video played. Jacobs and Matthews diligently worked on the HVAC units. With three hours in, we found nothing.

Governor Ortiz sat beside me. "Still nothing?"

"Nothing."

Ortiz asked the same question every hour, and I gave him the same reply. I requested a break, and Ortiz nodded to the operator, who paused the film. The governor stood and stretched.

"Chet, I have complete faith in you. If there's an anomaly, you'll find it."

"And if there isn't?"

His eyes locked on mine. "We'll cross that bridge when we get there." Ortiz cleared his throat. "If you'll excuse me, relocation plans need authorization."

Ortiz departed, and the operator allowed a five-minute recess. When I returned, Major Dixon, our head of security, had taken the governor's chair. He invited me to sit.

I opted to stand. "Play the reel."

The operator nodded and flipped a switch. Jacobs and Matthews moved between pieces of equipment. One knelt, another stood, while the other fiddled with a control panel. Another hour passed like this.

"There!" I saw the spark.

The operator paused the reel, and Dixon narrowed his eyes and drew closer to the screen. "Sabotage? Faulty equipment?"

I shook my head. "No way of knowing without a thorough investigation, and the unit won't be cool enough anytime soon."

Dixon stood, and his steely-eyed glare softened before he spoke.

"Be with your family. Get your rest. It'll be a long time before you can do anything like that again."

What that implied, I had no idea. Had Ortiz already decided my fate? Even if he had, it wouldn't be prudent to bring a member of security, the head or otherwise, in on a decision before further evidence surfaced. Anyone outside Ortiz's circle would only know an arrest had been made. Neither of those had happened. Heeding Dixon's advice, I headed home.

UNESCORTED as I trekked toward Zone Four, I breathed more freely. Glad of the silence, broken only by my footfalls, I put distance between myself and command.

My family awaited, likely with a bombardment of questions. But what would I tell them? There was an explosion in Zone Five. They already knew that.

The door to my unit opened, and my wife, Alena, stood before me. "What'll happen next?"

"I don't know."

Samantha and Jordan joined her in the living room, daughter and son flanking her.

I met Samantha's eyes, then Jordan's eyes. "Am I not allowed in?"

"I knew he wouldn't tell us anything." Samantha huffed and stomped away.

Alena smirked as she stepped toward me. "Sam's just worried about Nick. Since the explosion, she hasn't heard from him."

I wrapped my arms around Alena and kissed her. "We didn't lose any families housed in Zone Five," I spoke louder. "Sam, you don't have to worry about Nick and his family. They're just being relocated."

Jordan spoke. "Dad, what aren't you telling us?"

I gazed into Alena's eyes and stepped away. Sam had rejoined us and leaned with her arms crossed against the wall.

"Nothing we can share at this moment. Trust me, okay?"

Alena turned away from me and addressed Samantha and Jordan. "Dinner is in fifteen m. Go finish your studies."

Sam began to protest. "We already— "

"Listen to your mother," I said as I plopped myself upon the couch.

With a grumble, they walked away. Jordan cursed as he closed the bedroom door behind him. Sam glared at me with wide eyes before marching out of the front door and slamming it.

Alena wrung her hands and sighed. "I don't know how much longer they can handle being underground."

I chewed my bottom lip. I wouldn't give voice to my agreement. "Getting out too soon will expose us all to who knows what kind of toxins."

Alena sat. "I know, Chet. But things are set in motion now."

I nodded and whispered. "Not here, and not out loud."

She pulled back. "Then when?"

A moment passed. She pressed the topic further. "Do you think they suffered much?"

"Doubtful," I said.

I locked eyes with hers. Alena simultaneously shrank back and rose to her feet.

She forced a smile. "How about a drink?"

I didn't answer, but she got the hint. Alena turned her back to me and disappeared into the kitchen. A cupboard door creaked open, the water turned on, then off, and the microwave beeped four times before humming to life.

The sound gave voice to an image playing in my mind of two men, both of whom I hired and trained personally. Matthews, the younger, had a child on the way, while Jacobs, just a few years older than me, had already seen his kids off to college just before the eruption. Matthews wouldn't live to see his child grow up in a world of ash and toxins, while Jacobs would no longer mourn the children he'd been unable to save.

It should've been me in the mechanical room, the first to inhale the fumes, which would've swept me away into a dreamless sleep. Like Mathews and Jacobs, I'd've been consumed in flames with no time for my nerve endings to register pain. Alena would've understood. My children, not so much.

Alena returned and handed me a cup of tea. Steam rose from the mug, and I allowed its heat to warm my hands. I took a sip.

She sat. "Have they given you any further instruction?"

The ominous *They*. Not Ortiz and his skeleton of a government, and certainly not those in the bunker. The Surface Dwellers above — those who survived — didn't know me, my name, or what I had done. But a handful of unknowns, fewer than a thousand, and maybe even fewer than that, knew me. They'd recruited me and called themselves The Agency. In exchange for my coerced cooperation, they ensured my safety and that of my family if I did one small thing in the design. They called it an orchestrated flaw, one which marked the beginning of Phase One. Though today's explosion surprised me, I figured it was the sign The Agency told me to look for.

I set the tea down and met Alena's gaze. "They haven't communicated further instructions, and you know they wouldn't communicate that quickly. Besides, whatever comes next can't be done alone. There must be another operative on the inside. I'm sure of it."

Alena stood. "I'm sure it won't be long."

The front door opened, and Sam had a bounce in her step as she entered. "If you want to know, I found Nick in the commissary."

"That's great, sweetheart," I said. "How are he and his family adjusting."

Sam shrugged. "Okay, I guess. Mom, can I help you finish preparing dinner?"

Alena gave me a peck on the cheek before she and my daughter went into the kitchen.

I mourned the loss of my children's innocence. Parting ways with a boyfriend or girlfriend used to be a passing thing.

But not now, not in the wake of an explosion within the safe confines of a bunker.

That was my doing, and soon I'd drag my family into a conflict long in the making.

FRAGMENTED images of Jacobs' and Matthews' last moments plagued my dreams as I tossed and turned beside Alena that night.

They glanced at each other. Matthews said something, and Jacobs laughed in response. The spark flashed, bright and instantaneous. A ball of flame appeared and expanded. It consumed the bodies of the two men. Neither had time to react or even writhe in agony as the fire engulfed the rest of the equipment. Then came the blast and flames licking at my back.

Alena shook me and cried out. "They're at the door."

Someone pounded on the door and shouted. "Open up!"

I recognized the muffled cadence of the voice.

"Stay here," I told Alena as I arose from the bed. The pounding continued. When I reached the front door, I glanced behind me and saw Samantha and Jordan peering through the darkness.

"Shut the door and go back to bed," I hissed.

Samantha stuck out her tongue and let the door close with a thud.

I opened the front door.

With bags under his eyes and stubble on his face, Major Dixon flashed me a thin smile and brushed past me. "The council is digging into the circumstances surrounding your journey to Bunker Nine." Dixon sat and massaged his temples. "Do you have anything to drink around here?"

Alena chimed in. "I can make some tea."

Dixon waved her off. "Something stronger."

"You know we can't store liquor in our apartments," I said.

Dixon glanced at me and grinned. "Surely you smuggled in a stash."

I exchanged a glance with Alena and nodded. She retreated into the kitchen and flipped on the lights. I pulled up a seat across from Dixon and waited.

Why was the major really here? I didn't know him well enough to consider him an ally or an adversary. Until recently, my encounters with him consisted of listening to his security briefings in monthly meetings. Beyond that, our paths rarely crossed.

Dixon sat up and leaned toward me. "This bunker is a meticulously planned community. The creators spent trillions on designing every detail of it. The eight others are exact copies. After the explosion, communications between the other bunkers went down. We haven't been able to get them back up, but you know that already. This facility was supposed to be flawless, and a security breach would have been impossible. Unless, of course, the breach occurred sometime during construction."

Alena returned with a tumbler containing a double shot of bourbon. Dixon thanked her as he took the glass. In one gulp, he downed it and placed it on the table between us.

He sighed. "Wonderful."

"Did you need anything else, Major?"

"Nothing," the major said. "Please, Alena, join us."

Alena and I exchanged a glance. While my nerves reeled, her face appeared expressionless.

He chuckled. "Sit back, Chet. Relax. I've got something to show you."

He reached into his pocket and produced a rectangular casing about the size of an engagement ring box. As he opened it, he displayed a blue oblong object. I recognized it immediately.

I reached for the device, but Dixon pulled it away as he stood, closing the case and putting it away. "One other thing." Dixon offered me his hand, which I took. "I'll be in touch."

He saw himself out of the door, and I turned toward Alena. Silence passed between us for several minutes until we were certain no one lurked outside the door.

The Agency said messages with further directions would be delivered to me but never said how. Major Dixon could be the mode of delivery, or he could be something else altogether. Whatever the case, whether I could call Dixon, an ally or adversary was now inconsequential. Could I trust him? The oblong object within the box confirmed he, like myself, had been recruited by the same individuals who called themselves The Agency.

"Is that?" Alena asked.

I handed her the slip. As she examined it, Alena opened her mouth to speak just as something on the table caught my attention. I raised my finger to my lips and nodded toward the table, and the file Dixon had produced earlier.

I picked it up and assessed its weight. Opening it, I pulled out a single page containing a handwritten note.

Phase Two is beginning.

PHASE One entailed setting the stage for instability. We had been fortunate to have avoided the loss of human life, but the destruction of Zone Five cost billions of dollars. It also created an atmosphere of fear and uncertainty within the bunker. I hadn't known how Phase One would play out. I only knew what I had been told.

They had approached one evening well over ten years ago. They knew my work, even though I'd been employed as a government contractor for only a few years. At the time, I'd already advanced quickly in my department, overseeing installation projects designed for hundreds of years of stable and sustainable life underground should the need ever arise. Bunker Nine was one of many sites I'd visited. By design, it was the most technologically advanced.

When they approached me, I hadn't even considered the possibility of a future coup. Why would I? I was happily married with two young children. I was thinking of creating a future for them.

Alena and I had been enjoying an anniversary dinner, and Samantha and Jordan, six and four at the time, had been at home with a sitter. While not the fanciest of establishments, the restaurant served several options for three to five-course meals. When Alena and I arrived that night, the Maitre d' informed us they had reassigned us to a new table due to scheduling conflicts. They gave us an upgrade on the house. Alena was thrilled at the special treatment, especially when they escorted us to a private booth with a curtain.

I should've known that something was up. Like Alena, I didn't put up a fight. Instead, I played it like I had planned this little charade for her. Sometime into the second course, the curtain pulled back. Our meal was interrupted by two official, though mostly nondescript-looking individuals, one man, and one woman. I assumed they were government agents. Like something out of *Men in Black*, they wore matching suits and sunglasses. Neither took off their sunglasses. As the man sat, the woman glanced into the dining room before closing the curtains.

Neither my wife nor I had spoken. We were both too shocked, though I did muster the wherewithal to speak. The woman sensed this and held up her hand.

"Mr. and Mrs. Davis. We intend to disrupt this establishment. While essential for our survival, human life is not our primary concern in the immediate, and we will use deadly force if needed. We have to keep the bigger picture in front of us. Control and genetic perfection are primary, and we are conscripting you into our service."

They waited for that to sink in as Alena and I exchanged glances. I stood and laughed.

"Tell me this is some kind of joke."

The man held out his hand, producing nine blue oblong devices that fitted in his palm. "When the time is right, you'll receive instructions on what to do with these."

He pulled my hand toward his and passed off the devices. Once in my hands, I examined them more closely. They were matte blue and weighed a little more than a handful of paper clips. Turning one over, I discovered tiny ridge marks and held it up.

"Exactly what purpose do these serve?"

The man began again, "As I said—"

"These," the woman said, "will improve the overall function of the systems within each bunker."

"That's highly unlikely," I said. Standing, I turned to Alena. "I do believe it's time for us to go."

The woman stepped into our pathway. "Refusing us will not go well for you or your family."

The man stood. "But trust us when we tell you, you and your family will be safe if you do this one thing for us."

When they took their leave, Alena scrutinized the devices still in my hand. She pushed my hand away and took a step back.

"Chet, what have we gotten ourselves into? Control? Genetic purity?"

I folded the devices into a napkin and slid them into the inside pocket of my blazer.

"Your guess is as good as mine. We'll find out soon enough, I suppose."

Eight years later, near the completion of Bunker Nine, I received an unmarked envelope in my box at work. I squirreled it away until I got home, and my wife and children were asleep.

I slipped out of the covers and crept out to the garage where I had left the envelope secure in the glove box of my car. Seated, I popped the glove box open. With meticulous care, I slid the paper out of the envelope and unfolded it.

You are the initiator of Phase One. Install each device into the compressor units of the control HVAC system. Further instruction will follow, providing you survive the end of Phase One.

34

My heart raced as I reread the instructions. I thought of the ridged backs I'd run my fingers over dozens of times in the last few years. Would they really fit seamlessly into the compressor units? If so, they were chips designed for that express purpose, but I had yet to ascertain the function the chips served. The agents had referred to control and genetic purity, but how would these chips enable anyone to accomplish both?

"Why are you up so late?"

I turned to face Alena, who stood with arms crossed several feet away from me.

"A letter with further instruction." I handed the letter to Alena.

"The HVAC refers to the bunkers, right? You realize you could potentially sabotage the project and endanger future lives." Her brow furrowed.

I shrugged. "More likely, if I don't go through with this, it'll be our lives instead, and they'll find someone else."

Her face clouded. "We don't even know what they are planning or why."

Two years passed between the time I completed the installation of the devices and the eruption of Yellowstone. Another year passed underground, and I was promoted to chief engineer of Bunker Nine. In their test phases, the HVAC systems worked better than expected. Though I didn't tell my superiors, I suspected the devices had something to do with it.

What I didn't know then was that those devices would cause an explosion in Zone Five. I had assumed they simply improved the overall effectiveness of the HVAC systems. I couldn't have been more wrong.

Since the mechanical room explosion, we hadn't received word from the other bunkers, which left me to conclude eight similar explosions had occurred. Only some poor S.O.B. in the other bunkers would've likely been called, as I had been, but they would have been incinerated, along with any other victim trapped inside their zones.

Still, even at this stage, the plan had yet to be revealed. I realized more than ever that I was one of several pawns on a chessboard, too afraid to ignore an order.

WE operate in the shadows, often blind to the grand plan. Yet we follow unquestioningly. See this mission through.

The sweat from the palm of my hand soaked into the crumpled note I grasped as I marched toward Ortiz's office. Who was I kidding? I was just a pawn on the chess board, the ark. Still, even a pawn can be transformed into the most powerful piece on the board. I had to believe I could serve a higher purpose even as I floundered in the darkness.

Ortiz had summoned me to his quarters for a reason. A status update was due, but I resolved to let the governor know what was happening instead. I'd likely face a court-martial and death if I were lucky.

The steel catwalk beneath my feet betrayed my misgivings as my footsteps clanked unsteadily on my descent to level one of Zone Two, where Governor Ortiz awaited my arrival.

Once on the main floor, someone brushed against my shoulder. I glanced over, and Major Dixon's eyes met mine. I hadn't anticipated an escort.

"Listen—"

"Keep your eyes forward."

I returned my gaze toward Ortiz's quarters.

"Welcome to the new order." Dixon slipped something into my hand. "Discreetly pop this into your mouth before entering."

I stopped. "What is this?"

Dixon's eyes locked onto mine. "The difference between life and death."

Hi pivoted and continued forward toward Ortiz's quarters. I followed as we closed the distance from two hundred paces to one hundred, then the final fifty. What did I have to lose?

I feigned a cough and covered my mouth. The pill landed on my tongue. I nodded to one of two guards at Ortiz's door as the pill dissolved into a bittersweet liquid I swallowed. The guards opened the door, and Major Dixon and I entered.

Priceless paintings decorated the walls of Ortiz's quarters. Like a captain's quarters, it served as an office and residents. Though three times larger than the rest of the residential quarters, I didn't envy the lifestyle but mildly appreciated the artwork. On the walls, I recognized Salvador Dali's *The Sacrament of the Last Supper* and *Crocifisso*. I wondered if the originals hung on the walls or if these were perfect copies. Either way, both seemed simultaneously out of place and suitable for the living quarters of the man who governed a glorified fall-out shelter.

Dressed in a grey pinstripe and a brightly covered tie, Governor Ortiz entered from a door on the far side of the room. "Gentlemen, take a seat."

He gestured toward the Victorian-style furniture, likely transported from what was once the Governor's mansion.

Dixon and I sat, and I struggled to find a comfortable position. Ortiz didn't condescend to our level but chose to remain standing.

"Status update?" Ortiz asked.

Still uncertain why I had been summoned to this meeting, I glanced at Major Dixon. He nodded, and I spoke first.

"All systems are stable in the remaining four zones. Communication has yet to be re-established with our counterparts in the other eight bunkers." I cleared my throat. "But there is something else."

Dixon stood. "Sir. You're aware there is a faction among us planning a mutiny."

Ortiz shrugged it off while my heart raced. Had I come all this way to be outed by Major Dixon? I barely knew the man, and this shadow organization had yet to reveal itself truly. Ortiz wouldn't have believed me even if I confessed to planting the devices. I needed to get out of here, and I shifted forward in my seat. Dixon motioned for me to remain seated as he continued his speech.

"Governor, I am certain you are also aware of the dissatisfaction among the people. Each is closely monitored and what they whisper in the privacy of their homes speaks volumes. We are on the verge of unrest, and the recent lockdowns and mandatory curfews have done nothing to ease their restlessness."

The governor stood there a moment, staring blankly past us. Major Dixon slipped a hand into his pocket and pulled out a small rod, his thumb poised on a button. When Dixon raised the rod, the lone guard in the room moved to tackle him. The room filled with gas. I coughed violently and dropped to the floor until I breathed clean air. Besides me, Dixon did the same. I scrambled toward Ortiz and the guard.

Dixon pulled me back. "They're already gone."

As the air cleared, I saw the guard and Ortiz. Boils formed on their skin, and their hands clutched frozen at their throats.

"But why?"

"Your wife will explain. Follow me."

Before I could process the first part of Dixon's statement, he darted out the door. I did the same and found myself amid what I could only describe as an organized mob. Around me, the few guards on duty were either unconscious or being wrestled to the ground.

A siren blared, and lights flashed, bringing the chaos around me to a screeching halt. A familiar voice conveying poise and presence filled the space.

"Residents of Bunker Nine, your freedom is underway. You are asked to return to your quarters and await further instruction."

"Alena?"

Major Dixon turned toward me and grinned. "Just wait to see what we have in store for you."

Two sets of hands grabbed hold of my arms and pinned them behind my back.

"We've got to move," Dixon shouted.

The guards pivoted, then shoved me through the mob.

TIME stood still as I waited in what could only be described as a holding cell. Bare walls echoed my every movement. A steel door bared the way between me and the illusion of freedom beyond this room.

Major Dixon and two armed guards had escorted me to this room hours ago. I had recognized Gary, one of the guards from my rounds. His face, however, conveyed the look of hardened steel, and he barely glanced at me before he and his partner shoved me through the fray of the mob.

When they brought me to the holding cell where I awaited Dixon's promise to come to fruition, I racked my brain. They had placed me under arrest, of that, I was sure. Though I didn't pull the proverbial trigger, I also wasn't in a position to cast the blame on Major Dixon. I'd take the fall for Ortiz's death. God only knew how The Agency that had coerced me into this mess would react when they discovered I was no longer in play. It didn't matter; no one would believe me if I unveiled my unwitting involvement.

But was I so innocent? My engineering and HVAC training never once encountered those devices. I hadn't needed them to improve the bunker systems, and I certainly didn't protest. I still believed the bunkers held humanity's last hope. The air above would mean sudden death for some and prolonged and painful death for others. Humanity had cancer, emphysema, and COPD to look forward to, not to mention the unknowns.

Still, I had to get out of this holding cell and get my family out of this bunker. Correction, I had to get my children out of this bunker. I couldn't trust Alena after hearing her voice so clear and commanding over the PA system. Despite what I knew about the air quality above ground, I had to believe we could survive the trek to safety. The volcanic ash couldn't have impacted the northernmost parts of Canada and the southernmost parts of Mexico. We could settle down there, my kids and I, and leave my wife to this underground hell. Alena could have it.

She'd betrayed me — that I knew — but I didn't know the breadth or depth of that betrayal. Had I been a plaything in her hands all this time, moving to her every whim? Or did The Agency or some other faction group recruit her to oppose The Agency? The secrets I kept, I kept from others, but not from her. She had been there from the beginning, and she'd see this, whatever it was, through to the end.

But I'd fight her from every corner; I had to. Fuck control and genetic perfection. Fuck genetic diversity, too. Whoever *they* were could lie in the shit they'd created. They'd used me to build the perfect fall-out shelters capable of sustaining life for hundreds of years if it came to that. They'd also used me to destroy a good fifth of Bunker Nine and likely the other eight remaining bunkers.

I laughed, and the walls echoed my laughter.

Fuck humanity's survival as well. Humanity had to have survived somewhere beyond the reaches of Yellowstone's super volcano. The U.S., despite popular opinion, does not represent the whole of humanity, nor does humanity's hope rest on the survival of the U.S.

I had to find my kids, and we had to get above the ground. I'd planned for this possibility and had four respirators ready to go. The challenge was to get them.

The room echoed to the release of the steel door's bolt. The door opened, and Major Dixon entered. I stood, and my sudden movement sent the chair crashing to the floor.

Major Dixon grinned. "Please, Chet. We're here on a friendly visit. No need for dramatics. But I think it's time we were clear about a few things."

———————— ✝ꓕꓲꓶꓶꓶ ————————

"You better get talking," I shouted at Dixon.

He continued to grin, completely unfazed, as he directed his attention to the cell door. I followed his gaze until a woman entered.

She wore heels and a dark, finely pressed pants suit with a matching top. I didn't recognize her until she sat down in front of me, right beside Major Dixon.

I took a step forward. "Alena?"

Alena cleared her throat and averted her eyes toward Major Dixon, who nodded. She looked back at me and forced a tight smile.

"Listen, Chet," Alena began with some hesitation. "Please, you should sit for this."

Too stunned to protest, I did as my wife directed and picked up my chair and sat across from the pair. She reached her hand across the table in what I took to be an attempt to offer comfort or show a sign of solidarity. I didn't return the gesture.

Major Dixon cleared his throat. "I think it's time, don't you?"

Alena folded her hand into her lap and nodded. "Chet, you won't like what I'm about to tell you, so I need you—"

"Just get on with it," I said.

"Very well," Alena said. "The eruption. The government was prepared for it. That's why we built the bunkers. That's also why they trained you to be the best engineer for the project."

I swallowed hard. Alena's mouth moved, and she became ever increasingly more animated. Beside her, Major Dixon nodded as they exchanged occasional glances during the explanation as if they were coconspirators letting the victim of a long-running sick joke in on the fun they'd had. This wasn't a joke, and no one was having fun.

"Davis," Major Dixon said. "You've got to understand. The forced eruption was decades, maybe more, in the making. The government wanted a reset. Genetic purification and all that."

I slammed my fists onto the table and seethed, directing my rage at Alena. "Tell me. Was our marriage even real?"

Behind them, the doors opened. I rose to my feet as four armed guards swarmed up. Two flanked Dixon and Alena, and the other two restrained me.

Major Dixon rose. "Davis, your marriage isn't relevant anymore. We're braving a whole new world."

"What about those who are dead?" I shouted and wrestled against the guards who tightened their grips. "Alena! How long have you known?"

Alena and Dixon turned away from me.

"Did you set me up that night at the restaurant?"

Alena froze. She turned and faced me. "Chet, you fool. We were all set up. Can't you see that?"

"What does that even mean?"

Dixon turned to the guards. "Take him to a cell."

He and Alena exited without another glance at me. I shouted expletives at them through the closing doorway, but to no avail.

A guard nudged me. "Let's go, Mr. Davis."

I pushed him off. "I can walk by myself."

They led me through a dark but short corridor and into a colorless room, bare except for a cot and a pot.

The door slammed and bolted shut; my only thoughts were of my children. They were all I had in life that was certain, or were they a lie, too?

THAT night they left me alone. I couldn't gauge the passage of time.

Outside the cell, the bunker's artificial light mimicked the passage of time. One day, our leaders told us, one day we will be above ground, and we'll need to be acclimated to the passage of time. While we hardly had the equivalent, we adapted, and only time would tell if we would truly be ready for daylight again. I didn't have the luxury of daylight's cheap imitation in this cell.

Instead, time passed slowly as I counted the rhythmic flicker of light — a bulb, dimly lit, became a reprieve to my restless mind and growing hunger.

I projected my frustration and anger outward when hunger morphed into hunger pangs. Toward the agency that roped me in, toward Alena, who had untold secrets of her own, and toward the government for forcing the super-volcano's eruption. But, most of all, toward myself for allowing myself to be duped.

What had I hoped to gain? The salvation of my family? Saved for what? A lifetime of hard living below ground? Or perhaps struggling against scorched earth and ash while fending off savages, taking advantage of the lawless state that would become the U.S.?

I scoffed, and my voice echoed mockingly. Then I realized I no longer hungered. I had endured the pangs of starvation, and I had endured the solitude. Death beckoned me, and I would soon be its guest.

Nonetheless, mental clarity rushed over me. My kids needed me, and I knew how to get out of here.

The cell door creaked open, and I shielded my eyes from the light that flooded the room. Two silhouettes approached.

A voice like gravel chuckled. "Looks like he has risen."

The other squatted and effortlessly pulled me to my feed. "Can you stand?"

"Yes," I croaked.

One of them handed me a canteen and a few crackers. I snatched them from his hands and guzzled half the glass before he stopped me.

"After all that time," he said. "You'll need to take small sips."

I set the glass down and wiped my mouth. "How long?"

"A few days," one said, and the other contradicted him with, "A few weeks."

"We haven't been here long," the second guard said.

The other ground out another response. "Follow us."

They turned and walked away without so much as waiting for a question. I had about one hundred of them.

We followed a familiar maze of catwalks and tunnels integrated throughout the entire bunker. I didn't need an escort as they took me to Zone Five, where the once-sealed doors stood open.

Beyond these doors, hundreds of uniformed men and women loaded gear onto armored vehicles or busied themselves in some fashion as they carried stamped boxes from one end of the zone to another.

One of the guards gave me a gentle shove, and I didn't need further prompting. Not until they led me to a makeshift office space where a woman typed vigorously on the computer.

I noted the single camera mounted in the corner of the room. The woman turned and smiled at me. Alena.

SHE motioned for me to sit down. Folding her hands and placing them on the desk, she spoke with a forced smile.

"Chet, I trust you're being treated well."

I shrugged. "Considering my wife had me locked up in a goddamn cell."

She dismissed the guards. When they had left, she leaned closer to me. "I don't like this any more than you do, so if you cooperate, we can move past all this."

Resisting the urge to slap her, I took a deep breath. "To what end?"

She picked up a remote and dimmed the lights. I didn't trust her, but I had to go along with her plans. A projector screen lowered from the ceiling to our right, where an image of a metropolis appeared.

"You're looking at what remains of the U.S. Government. As we both know, it must be eliminated if we are to survive."

"I assume the 'we' are those who possess the genetic diversity for repopulation."

She nodded. "And our family."

I doubted that included me, but I had to know what she had planned. "I'm one man."

"You're the perfect trigger man," Alena corrected me.

I scoffed. "Or the perfect chump."

She ignored my comment and clicked the remote. An armory appeared on the screen. "Our sources tell us the last of our nation's leadership is hunkered below ground."

"And you want me to do what exactly?"

She handed me a dossier. "We need a hard reset."

The plan was simple. Head northeast, get inside as an HVAC man, and plant a few explosives. Then skedaddle before the whole thing blows. It was a shit plan that didn't guarantee my survival. Not that I expected it to. Anarchy rarely comes with guarantees. Still, going along with the plan would buy me some time.

"I leave at 0200."

She nodded. "I assume you accept."

What the hell? I nodded my consent.

"Good," Alena said as she stood.

I did the same as she walked around the desk. Flinging her arms around me, she planted her lips on mine. She smelled of lilacs, and my lips gave way to hers. As suddenly as she initiated our exchange, she pulled away. Her eyes, filled with passion and pleading, met mine.

She had maneuvered us, so I stood between her and the camera's line of sight. She mouthed the words, *Get the* children. As she came onto me once more, I returned her passionate kisses.

———————— ✗⊼⎟⎟⨎⨎ ————————

FOUR hours until departure didn't leave me much time. I passed through corridors and crossed over catwalks as I headed toward our family's apartment. Though I didn't know the full extent of Alena's involvement with The Agency or her apparent double cross, I had to trust she had our children's best interests in mind. Maybe she'd gone in too deep, or maybe her display of passion was just an act.

I flipped through the dossier again. At best, I would shake up what was left of the U.S. government and send them swarming throughout the countryside, uprooting The Agency dead set on toppling them. I could make it through the front doors of the armory and find my way into the central hub of the HVAC systems. The Agency, or Alena, chose me precisely because I had the credentials and clearances. I could do it, but my involvement would gain nothing and cost me everything. Saving my children and getting the hell out of this bunker was a better option. And 0200 fast approached.

"Kids," I called out as I barged through the apartment door. "Sam? Jordan?"

"Here," Jordan hissed.

He and Sam sat on the couch. Beside Sam sat her boyfriend, Nick. The three of them held small bags in their laps.

"Mom said it's okay if he comes," Sam said, nudging herself closer to Nick.

I thought of the access panel in Zone One and the items I had stashed away.

"Fine," I said. "Mom'll have to catch up with us later."

The kids nodded, and we waited until darkness set over the bunker and the last chime of the night rang out, signaling curfew.

I nodded to the kids, and they followed me to the back of the apartment, where we surrounded a small utility closet. A stack of seven boxes made very little room for general maintenance work. But that mattered very little. Access to the panel behind the boxes would open up to a maze of interconnecting ductwork and tunnels, all of which would lead us to Zone One and our freedom.

Jordan, Sam, and Nick assisted in the removal and relocation of the boxes while I loosened the panel and placed it to the side of the opening.

I turned to the kids. "Climb up and move to the right and wait for me. Once I'm up, you'll follow me."

They nodded and climbed through the opening. As I stuck my head through the opening, a pounding came at the front door. I cursed under my breath. Either the night watchman had spotted the lights on in the hallway, or someone waited outside to see me off to complete my mission to topple the skeletal remains of the U. S. Government.

I switched off the light and waited. Silence ticked off the moments, and I stepped inside the utility closet and closed the door behind me. After crawling through the opening, I did my best to slide the panel back in place. I didn't test its security. I only hoped it held long enough for us to make our escape.

I climbed up, hung a left, and behind me, the kids eased their way over the opening below and followed. We had only to endure the heat and tedious nature of pausing to keep from alerting the patrol below to our movement above.

Hours passed without commotion from the residents and guards below. I checked the time: 0030. The dossier indicated I would need to be at the main gate by 0200. That gave us an hour's head start if we didn't hit any snags in the next half hour. I only hoped the ash had settled enough at this point to keep us from leaving footprints to mark our escape.

BELOW me, a guard paced back and forth on the outermost point of Zone One. For what purpose? Only I knew of the stash of supplies I'd hidden behind the access door just out of our reach. It was possible Alena had tracked my movements all this time, but to what end? Especially with the safety of our children on the line.

Behind me, one kid shifted their weight and sent sound ricocheting off the walls. We froze as the guard looked up and waited.

Mercifully, the clanging from above began again. Below us, the guard cursed and moved on. I shimmied forward until I reached a cornered-off section where a vent opened to a chamber wherein my supplies lay untouched and tucked away. As I looked over my shoulder, three sets of eyes filled with expectation met mine. I nodded. Popping the vent open, I crawled out. I turned to help Jordan, Sam, and Nick out and led them on hands and knees toward our supplies.

I pulled out four packages of masks and handed them out. I did the same with goggles and explained, "You'll need to wear these at all times. Or until we can be sure the air is safe."

They nodded and donned masks and goggles. I slipped a bag over my shoulder and showed the kids they should do the same. From proper protection to packaged food and access to clean water, these bags would be sufficient until we made it outside the radius of soot and ash that likely covered the desert above.

Motioning for the kids to follow as I shuffled to the access door above, I cranked the hand wheel to the left and one lock released. I continued to turn the wheel until I heard three more clicks and a gentle hiss. The door popped open, and I shielded my eyes from the light above. The kids did the same.

Somehow, we'd lost track of time below ground. I climbed out, quickly aware of my mistake. Flood lights mounted on the top of two military-style Humvees marked our location. A figure, silhouetted by the lights, approached.

"Mr. Davis?" the figure asked.

I raised my right hand in a wave.

"Let me guess?" I asked. "Phase Three?"

Behind me, Sam spoke. "Dad, what's going on?"

"Fuck me," the figure said. "You brought your kids?"

I nodded, and the figure sighed.

"Come along, then," the figure said. He turned and walked toward the Humvee. We followed.

AS daylight broke through the cloud of ash still layering the surrounding air, I glimpsed remnants of a once proud country we'd never see again. A toppled monument here and a crumbling state house there. Even outside the uninhabitable epicenter of Yellowstone's eruption, much of the country remained desolate.

From the side of the road, a grimy child stood by his mother, who rooted through a pile of rubble. When we passed, he waved at us. I waved back. In the backseat, Jordan, Sam, and Nick wore expressions of empathetic suffering. This would be their inheritance. Not the glossy malls or the clean parks where families drove their vans for a picnic. No, they would inherit ash and rubble if they remained in this country.

North into Canada was where we should go, where evergreen trees still thrived, though the climate was likely ten to twenty degrees cooler than it should be. Or perhaps we ought to go south into Mexico. That would force us to pass through the epicenter of the eruption again. But would the Mexican borders be open to citizens of an America that ceased, long before the eruption, to offer hope and refuge to the tired, poor, and huddled masses yearning to breathe freely?

Only time would tell. Until then, I had a job to do. I understood that now. I turned to our driver, the figure who greeted us weeks ago. "How much longer?"

"Another day's drive," he said. "But know you're not doing this alone."

Ahead of us, another caravan of Humvees pulled onto the otherwise barren interstate highway.

Our driver turned to me and grinned. "That should be your counterpart from Bunker Seven."

I nodded.

More would come, of that I was certain. We would raze the final remains of an America built upon the tyranny of the fat cats and politicians of DC and Wall Street. From the ash and rubble, we would rebuild and live free.

Locked In

Now

I CATCH MY BEARINGS and peer through the midday rush of students anxiously getting to their lockers. I should be doing the same, but I need to find Clara. A second ago, she passed by the lunchroom. Then the bell rang, and she was gone.

My bro Trey joins me. "Thought you could use some help."

I know what he's thinking—with the day half over and everyone ramped up, I need to tell her now.

"Yo," Trey nods toward the end of the hallway.

I glance over my shoulder. Clara maneuvers through a crowd of students toward me. She wears hip-hugging jeans and a pink halter top.

"Is she—"

"She is," Trey says. He claps me on the shoulder. "Gotta bounce. You've got this!"

Clara approaches. I can't help noticing a streak of dark makeup beneath her eyes.

"Hi, Seth," she says, taking a step closer. I catch a whiff of strawberries and vanilla.

"What's going on?" I ask.

Clara's lips part. I take a deep breath.

Loud bangs echo down the hallway behind me, bouncing off the lockers, making the noise even crazier. Suddenly, everyone's freaking out as they respond to the popping and ringing. Terror passes over Clara's face; I grab her hand.

"This way!"

Around us, our classmates stampede in every direction. Up ahead, I spot Mr. Brown, our biology teacher, ducking into his classroom while shutting the door. I slip beneath his arm.

We're safe!

On Mr. Brown's command, we slide tables and chairs against the door and close the blinds. The lights flicker off just as we crouch in the single corner designated with a red sticker.

I snort and mumble, "'The fortress.' But are we locked in or locked out?"

Mr. Brown glares at me as he puts his index finger over his lips. Someone's phone buzzes, which pisses him off.

"Do you think this is a drill?" He hisses. "Silence! Cell phones off!"

Inside, the steady breathing of my classmates is oddly calming. Outside, the hallways become silent. No more gunshots, no more chattering. The clock on the wall ticks away. Footsteps echo outside the room. Is it one set or two?

Someone in the room whimpers. The doorknob jiggles. My heart thuds in my chest.

Clara!

Just when I had her, I blew it. I couldn't keep her out of danger. I rise and grit my teeth.

Earlier that Day

CHEAP COLOGNE AND FRUITY body spray mingle with that unmistakable under-armpit smell. Lockers click and jiggle as they open and close. The entire student body fills the hallway, creating a constant buzz of chatter around me.

Trey joins me as I fiddle with my locker. "You've got this, right?"

I tighten my lips. "Sure."

"No offense," Trey says. "But you're overthinking it. Just ask her."

"I will," I say. "I'm waiting for the right moment."

The hallway vibe suddenly shifts, and I spin around.

A crowd of students seems to part before a trio of girls led by Clara. She smiles and waves at me, wiggling her fingers as she does so. I freeze as my throat goes dry and my face heats up.

"Hey," I croak.

When she passes by, her long black hair against her pale smooth skin waves behind her.

Knuckles drive a wedge of pain into my shoulder.

"Dude!" I whine as I turn. "What'd you do that for?"

"You're missing your moment."

Trey flashes a broad, goofy grin and nods toward the girls. Clara's hips sway, and she swipes a strand of hair over her shoulder. Her profile comes into view, and I swear she sees me.

"Nah, man," I say. "What if she's just being friendly?"

Trey blows air through tight lips. "Ask her."

The bell rings.

Trey and I bump fists and split. Disappearing into the chaotic crowd headed to our first-period classes, I search the sea of faces, hoping to catch another glimpse of her. If I could lock eyes with Clara again, I'd muster up the courage to ask her out today.

Still, I hesitate. What if Clara doesn't give me another thought? I've wasted six months on these endless what-ifs. Trey has a point. I'm overthinking it.

I brush past a group of students still lingering in the hallway. One says something about schools closing early.

"Highly unlikely," I mutter

First Period, Government

FIRST PERIOD: BIOLOGY, room 101.

Second period: English, room 232.

Third period: Phys. Ed.

I tap the eraser end of my pencil on the desk and stare at the remaining gaps where I've penciled in a few possibilities for Clara's fourth and fifth periods. She has her government class during her sixth period and art class during her seventh period. I know this because I once saw her enter those wings while I took a detour between class changes.

"Seth Roland!"

I stiffen, and the room goes silent.

Ms. Heller glares at me—someone snickers. The kid next to me shifts uncomfortably in their seat.

"Sorry. What's the question?"

"Can you tell us about one economic or political factor that led to World War II?"

My throat tightens. I silently count down from ten. I swallow hard. Breathing out slowly, I slump in my seat.

A girl from the back of the room spouts an answer. Ms. Heller thanks her and asks another question.

Is she still on the same topic? I'm pretty sure she hasn't moved on.

I raise my hand.

Ms. Heller pauses her instruction to call on me. "Yes, Seth."

"Aggression by totalitarian powers?"

Even though I am sure of the answer, I speak it like a question.

With narrowed eyes, Ms. Heller nods. She takes a deep breath and lets it out slowly. "Thank you for that." Turning, she directs her attention to the rest of the class. "Now, when I call your names, move to your designated stations..."

A wad of paper hits the back of my head. Though I choose to ignore it, my neck burns.

Ms. Heller calls my name, and I shuffle toward a corner of the room where three others—Becky, Dan, and Lara—have already taken their seats. I do the same while a stack of papers slides from one desk to another.

I don't really know these kids, but I hope they'll let the next fifteen minutes slip away without further commentary.

After reading our assigned research question, Lara coos. "I know just what we need to do!"

She launches into an explanation I only half listen to.

When the bell rings, Ms. Heller approaches me. I pretend not to notice as I grab my things and dip. She calls my name, but I am already out the door.

Dashing toward the gymnasium, I don't bother taking a detour by Clara's second-period classroom. I've already tried every imaginable route to run into her. The combination of these resulted in a D for Phys. Ed. because I was way too late and didn't bother to change.

Third Period, English

I STARE AT THE DISTORTED red figure of a merry-go-round horse on the cover of J. D. Salinger's famous work. No one talks about his other works, just like I hope no one talks about last period's incident.

Thirty minutes ago, I felt like that horse, wildly bucking with my face in another guy's sweaty armpit. I didn't sign up for wrestling, yet there I was, quickly letting him pin me down so I could get my sorry ass off the mat. Despite the rinse down and half a can of body spray, I can still smell the other guy's funk on me.

I flip to chapter two as our teacher, Mrs. Jackson, reads.

"Life is a game, boy. Life is a game that one plays according to the rules."

When she finishes, she marks her place in the book with a finger and closes it while asking the predictable question. "What's going on here? What does this conversation between Holden and Spencer reveal?"

It's not a difficult question, and I wonder if she realizes how simple the answer is. Like Holden, we must follow the rules to navigate the world successfully. The problem is no one wants to volunteer the obvious.

I shoot my hand up. Mrs. Jackson nods in my direction.

"Here's the thing," I begin. "Holden feels alone because he understands life's a game with rules. He also understands there are going to be winners and losers. The problem is that he hasn't been given the 'rule book'" —I use air quotes— "Or, if he has, he doesn't agree with the rules because the rules suck."

A girl chimes in, saying something very similar. She adds the less-than-original idea that Holden thinks everyone is a phony.

I envy Holden for having the courage to think it's all bullshit. Tapping my pencil, I flip open my notebook and stare at what I've scratched out of Clara's schedule. She doesn't have lunch with me, so she must have Math or Tech during her fifth period. Phys. Ed. never takes place during that painfully long fifth block.

With a quick detour, I could risk running into Clara before the fourth period. That could work if I hung out in the main hallway.

Would Holden call me a phony?

Probably. Clara is way out of my league. I know it. She must know it. My thoughts spiral down to a dead end where I face a simple reality. At best, Clara and I have spoken five, maybe six, times.

Still, she's given me the time of day. I can't be that much of a phony. She's already made the pass; I just have to volley it back. Easy!

When the bell finally rings, I'm the first out the door. I don't bother pushing my chair in or putting away any borrowed classroom materials.

Fourth Period

"YO, SETH!"

Trey, a head taller than almost everyone else, approaches through the crowd. I swallow down my frustration. We bump fists.

Trey smirks. "You skipping class or something?"

I spot Clara slipping into the counseling office and tilt my head in that direction.

"I saw her," Trey says. "But I think your stalking's got her all worked up."

"No way she could've noticed," I retort.

"Bro, she's noticed."

My phone vibrates in my pocket. Taking it out, Trey does the same with his.

This is County Police reporting an active shooter near Cross Road and Taylor Drive. Avoid Area or Run, Hide, Fight. Stay tuned in for updates.

I barely have time to register this news when the intercom cuts on.

"Attention staff and students. This is a code yellow. Teachers, please close and lock all doors and continue instruction. Students report to the nearest classroom or office."

The counseling office door opens, and one guidance counselor motions for us to come inside. Once in, he locks the door.

"Names?" He asks.

We tell him, which prompts him to a workstation where I guess he marks us present. I take a seat facing the rest of the counseling office. Of the four interior offices, Mrs. Mack's door is closed. Clara must be in there for a meeting.

Trey and I check our online school app and discover nothing worth our attention. Is anyone bothering to do any work? More than likely, everyone—including teachers —is shooting a text to friends and family.

Trey and I get sucked into social media and games for what seems like hours. I pour past streams of speculation, none of which indicates whether the threat has passed. Still, Mrs. Mack's door remains closed. At this point, I don't think she's even in there.

I nudge Trey. "Did you see Clara leave?"

He shrugs. "Maybe she went to class when we received the alert."

The intercom cuts on, and we receive instruction that the code yellow is over. We stand, and Clara opens the office door. When our eyes meet, she inhales deeply, and a tear trickles down her cheek. Passing us by, she exits into the hallway.

"Smooth," Trey says.

I can't tell if he's being sarcastic or affirming my decision to let her alone.

Lunch

DESPITE "NORMAL" ACTIVITIES resuming after the lifting of the code yellow and the downgraded police warning, the lunchroom still buzzes about the supposed shooter.

A girl turns to a group of friends and shows them her phone. "See! My friend is in the next school district. He says the police are still searching for him."

I overhear a conversation behind me. "Yeah? My cousin says it's over. He's a senior."

"Don't prove anything," someone else says. "Besides, there's photo evidence."

The friend pushes the phone away. "I'm eating."

I had yet to hear anything verifiable. Local news outlets, if we can trust them, still report the shooter is on the loose with no casualties to the elementary school the shooter, or shooters, targeted.

To be honest, it's terrifying. Everyone around me is super casual about the whole thing.

Correction.

Clara passes by the cafeteria with a slow heaviness in her gait.

Trey nudges me. "You gonna catch up to her, or what?"

I put my fork down and stand. "I'm doing this."

Brushing past a few students and ignoring the call of an administrator, I head straight toward the cafeteria door. A teacher in the hallway attempts to question me about my business while I swivel in search of her.

The bell rings, and the chaos sweeps me away.

Now

I GRIT MY TEETH AND survey the fortress we've created out of this room. Some students rock with their backs pressed against the wall. Catching my gaze, they avert their attention elsewhere. A girl huddles in the corner and sniffles. She brings her knees to her chest, crosses her arms, and rocks. Even Mr. Brown does his best to hide beneath the teacher's desk, but his leg shakes nervously. How did I let go of Clara's hand? Where is she?

None of this makes any sense. We've barricaded the doors, but for what? We can either sit here and wait to be picked off until help arrives or take action. Choosing the latter, I grab the closest thing I can use as a weapon—a biology textbook.

Mr. Brown hisses. "Seth. Get down!"

I go to the window and peek through the blinds. Police emergency lights dance red and blue, and a S.W.A.T. team has already taken position. A series of gunshots go off somewhere on the other side of the building. Maybe upstairs, but nowhere near us. No one outside appears to be in a hurry to breach the building. Did they even hear the gunshots?

I turn toward the others in the room. "We can't stay here forever. The police aren't even attempting to get inside. We'd be safer out there."

Without waiting for a response, I march toward the door. Mr. Brown makes no attempt to stop me. Like a handful of others, he tries to crouch further into the recesses of a desk.

One, a boy, stands.

"You're right. We need to do something."

I nod and set the textbook down. "We'll have to clear this."

As we do, one by one, our classmates join in. Shoving a desk to the side, then a chair, I wonder if others are like me. People who are swearing they'll tear down the so-called rules, throw off the doubt and fear, and get out of hiding.

With the door clear, I take the lead and pick up the textbook. I don't know what good it'll do me, but at least it's something. I crack the door open and listen. The hallway greets me with eerie silence. Still, I wait.

Gunfire pops off. I turn. My classmates have ducked, but I motion we should keep moving. I dash toward the stairwell and lead the descent. Several feet squeak and echo off the concrete walls and linoleum flooring.

When I reach the bottom of the steps, I slam the emergency exit open and hold the door as my classmates exit.

Five officers dressed in tactical gear approach. One takes hold of the door and says, "Good job, son. Join the others."

I tighten my lips and follow my classmates. A team of officers, their weapons lowered, break rank and lead us past the safety of the police line. Once there, I frantically look around. Teachers, including Mr. Brown, lead their students away from danger. While I'm glad he worked up the courage to get out, it would've been nice if he'd taken the lead.

Upon spotting Clara standing just beyond several news crews, I dash toward her and push past adults and teens, oblivious to my speedy approach.

But Clara sees me and offers me a weak smile. Her two friends follow her gaze. One raises her eyebrows at me. The other embraces Clara and gives her a peck on the cheek.

A lump catches in my throat.

When the two depart, I approach Clara and attempt an apology.

"When the gunshots went off, I thought you were behind me. I'm sorry."

She shakes her head. "I thought you were going toward the exit, but you pulled away fast. The crowd dragged me off and out the front door after that."

My cheeks burn. "I'm glad you made it to safety."

"I'm glad you made it out, too," she says.

I want to ask her out, but that seems inappropriate. "How are you holding up?"

She picks at a fingernail. "Not good. You saw me in guidance, right?"

I nod, not knowing what else to say.

"Before everything went down, I found out my cousin was planning something. I had to tell counseling. I was about to tell you, but everything happened so fast."

I struggle for the right response. *That's horrible. I'm here for you.* Neither response seems right.

As we take each other in, Mrs. Mack approaches us. "Clara, I'm sorry to interrupt, but your parents are here."

Clara sniffles and nods to her. "Thanks, I'll be right there."

When Mrs. Mack walks away, Clara turns to me. "I heard about what you did in there. That was very brave."

"Thanks," I say. "Um... Clara. I'm here if you need a friend or someone to talk to."

"I know, Seth. Thanks." She takes my hand and squeezes it.

Just before disappearing into the crowd, Clara turns with a nod. I return the gesture.

All of us made it safely. Someone thanks me for getting some students out. Still, I don't feel very brave.

"Seth!" Trey shouts as he jogs over, slinging his arm around my shoulder. "They caught the guy, and everyone is calling you a hero! What you did in there was freaking amazing!"

I shrug. "I dunno. I just grabbed a book and dipped."

"Nah, man! I saw you chatting it up with Clara. You totally rocked it."

Even though I'm doubting myself deep down, I must admit Trey's right. I acted heroically, and everyone was safe because I played my part. I only hope to carry that over into a relationship with Clara. But for now, she'll need the time with her family and time to heal. I get that. But when she comes back, I'll be there for her.

The Unwanted Guest

CHEYENNE jostled about in the front passenger seat of the orange Jeep Wrangler as it turned down an unpaved road marked *Twin Peaks Resort*. She took in the sites as gravel crunched beneath off-road tires. Prefabricated trailers trying to pass themselves off as rustic cabins sat in an alcove to the left. A community pool to the right already hosted late afternoon campers.

"You've got to be kidding," Cheyenne grumbled as she turned to Katrine.

Katrine's smirk sharpened her elegant figure. "Keep an open mind, love. We've squirreled ourselves away from civilization all summer. Sometimes a girl just needs —"

"Creature comforts," Cheyenne cut her off with a roll of her eyes. "You've told me this a million times."

Katrine glanced at Cheyenne and grinned. "Live a little, will ya?" She punched the gas and sent the Jeep bouncing over a bare patch of road. The women laughed.

Some would say their mutual love of outdoor adventure brought them together; others would say opposites attract. Katrine was tall, tan, and athletic, wearing her hair in a short pixie cut while favoring equally short and revealing clothing. On the other hand, Cheyenne favored baggy clothing and maintained long, dark dreadlocks that cascaded down to the small of her back. Her face was pale, round, and delicate, with a pinkish hue to her cheeks.

Katrine parked the Jeep outside the campground office. While Katrine checked in, Cheyenne climbed out and stretched. Squeals of children playing on a nearby playground carried through the air while the voices of parents calling their children for dinner echoed in the distance. *Twin Peaks Resort* was a far cry from the last four places she and Katrine camped. Those places were remote, and Cheyenne preferred it that way. Her guess was as good as any why Katrine chose this location, but Cheyenne had her money on the pool.

A steel door slammed shut, and Cheyenne turned to see Katrine approach with a bounce in her step.

"It's your lucky day," she said, waving papers. "We're in lot C23, far away from all this. Shall we, love?"

Cheyenne stepped over to Katrine, and the two exchanged a quick peck on the lips. "We shall," she said.

AFTER navigating through a maze of narrow dirt roads that snaked through a dense forest, the Jeep stopped.

Katrine cursed. "You've got to be kidding."

Cheyenne followed Katrine's gaze. A faded blue tent was pitched in the neighboring lot, and a similarly aged pick-up sat idling in the driveway.

"Yay," Cheyenne said with feigned enthusiasm.

"You don't get it," Katrine said. "The couple at the office said no one else would be down here."

A young man with unkempt shoulder-length hair got out of the pick-up, glanced their way, and then hurried over to the firepit at his campsite.

Cheyenne's throat tightened. "We could go to a different site."

Katrine pulled the Jeep forward, then backed it into the campsite. "Let's just pitch the tent, then let the front office know about this unregistered guest of theirs."

With the vehicle in park, Cheyenne climbed out. As Cheyenne stood to unhook the luggage rack, she heard Katrine call, "Hiya, neighbor!"

Cheyenne peered through the windows, catching a glimpse of Katrine waving. "What're you doing?"

"What do you think?" Katrine hissed without turning around.

Leaving the luggage for later, Cheyenne joined Katrine on the other side of the Jeep. Their neighbor stood next to a picnic table some thirty yards away. A spatula dangled loosely in his hand, and he stood staring at Katrine.

"Maybe he's deaf," Cheyenne offered, just loud enough for the young man to hear her if the opposite were true.

The man shifted his weight from one foot to another. From this distance, it was hard to tell where his eyes landed, but she knew men well enough, and his silence made her skin crawl.

To make matters worse, Katrine adjusted her bikini top, one of two nervous ticks she had. The second was rambling. "We just came in from another campground a few hundred miles away," Katrine said. "Beautiful drive. We're making a tour of the tri-state area. You know, hit up all the campsites before returning to the old grind."

Cheyenne detected a hint of playfulness in Katrine's voice and nudged her. "Stop it."

Katrine shrugged, then continued. "It's lovely here, but we're out of booze and beer. Do you know of any good places to hang?"

"Yeah," the man's voice cracked. He averted his gaze and cleared his throat. "I hang here all summer, and there's this bar the locals go to."

"Awesome," Cheyenne said dryly. She grabbed Katrine by the arm. "Babe, we've got to set up camp and —" She paused, then whispered. "This guy's giving me the creeps, and I'm sure he's been staring at you this entire time."

Katrine blushed, and her eyes grew wide. She forced a smile and waved at the man. "Maybe we'll see you around."

"Yeah," the man grinned. "Around."

Both women turned back to the Jeep. Cheyenne shivered as she imagined the man staring at them as they walked away. It was all she could do not to look back to confirm her suspicions.

Katrine hoisted herself onto the Jeep and reached for a duffle bag. "Cheyenne, help me with this, will ya?"

Cheyenne tied her dreadlocks back. "After you put something on."

"On?" Katrine asked. She glanced down at herself. "I'm wearing a top and these jean shorts you insisted I wear. If anything, you should dress down a bit."

Cheyenne crossed her arms and hinted with her eyes toward the weirdo in the neighboring campsite. "Have you not noticed? He's still looking at us."

When Katrine glanced at the neighboring campsite, the man spun, and the spatula landed in the campfire. He crouched, attempted to retrieve it, then recoiled his hand.

Katrine stifled a laugh. "I'm sure he's harmless, love."

Cheyenne crossed her arms. "And if he isn't?"

"I'll have the .38 loaded and ready to go," Katrine said. "Now, are you gonna help me, or do I have to set up camp by myself?"

"I'm helping," Cheyenne sighed.

The women unloaded camping gear from the Jeep and quickly set up the two-person tent. While Katrine popped into the tent to lay out their sleeping arrangements, Cheyenne busied herself as she tied a tarp over the picnic table.

"Hi!" the young man's voice cracked.

Cheyenne jumped and turned, dropping the rope and the corner of the tarp. Somehow, he'd gotten within ten feet of her, and she hadn't noticed. She took a deep breath.

"Sorry about that," the man said. "Do you need any help?"

He crossed over to Cheyenne and leaned over, reaching for the rope while his dark, greasy hair fell forward. Cheyenne snatched the rope up before he could grab it. She stepped away.

"Thanks, anyway," Cheyenne said. "Listen, I'm not trying to be rude or anything. The front office said —"

The man waved her off. "I'm here all the time. They're very disorganized. Here," he seized a loose end of the tarp. "Let me help you with this."

Cheyenne bumped into the picnic table as she tugged at the rope. "I've got this. Besides, my wife and I are expert campers. I've set up hundreds of these."

The man nodded but didn't let go of the tarp. Instead, he glanced around the campsite. "I'm a bit of an expert camper, myself. This is my fourth campground this summer. I'll be leaving tomorrow for a more remote area."

If he was taken aback by Cheyenne's claim on Katrine, he didn't show it.

"Right," Cheyenne said. "Didn't you say you hang out here all summer?"

"Did I?" he asked. "I meant I come here all the time. I like the rustic feel."

"The bathhouses have modern plumbing, and there's an electrical hook-up right over there." She pointed to the cased-in outlets protruding from the ground between their campsites.

The man laughed. "Not your thing, huh?"

"For the amateurs," Cheyenne said, sitting on the tabletop to appear more comfortable. "We're more the survivalist types. Prepared for anything, if you know what I mean."

"I think I do," the man said. He glanced over her shoulder at the tent. "You sure you don't need help?"

Cheyenne followed his gaze. The tent shook, and its wall bulged slightly as Katrine moved around inside. Cheyenne stood and stepped into the man's line of sight.

"Listen," Cheyenne said with the warmest smile she could offer. "Thanks for stopping over, but there's a bit more we need to do to finish up before dinner and nightfall."

He raised his gaze to hers. Cheyenne studied his face for the first time, noting his deep-set brown eyes and the acne scars on his skin, likely due to an old habit he acquired from his angsty teenage years.

"If you ladies need anything, give ol' Rico a holler." He chuckled and gestured toward his campsite. "I'll be right over there."

Cheyenne crossed an arm over her chest and waved. "Bye, Rico."

Rico lingered there for a moment, then he added. "Just be careful, is all. As you suggested, this campground may seem like a resort, but you never know what'll happen after midnight."

"That's oddly specific," Cheyenne said.

"Just keep an eye out," Rico said, then dropped the tarp and sauntered back to his dwindling campfire.

When Cheyenne saw he was out of sight—and likely out of hearing distance—she darted to the tent and practically ripped open the flap.

Katrine screeched and snatched up a towel.

"Why are you half-naked?" Cheyenne hissed.

"I'm getting into something more practical," Katrine said. She lowered her eyelids and purred. "Do you want to join me?"

"Under normal circumstances, yes," Cheyenne said as she stepped inside and zipped up the flap.

Katrine let the towel drop and grabbed a sports bra. "So, how's ol' Rico?"

Cheyenne's eyes widened. "You heard all that?"

Katrine knelt beside her bag and rearranged the contents. "I heard enough."

Cheyenne plopped down beside her. "I'm telling you, there is something off about that guy."

"Maybe he doesn't get out much," Katrine offered. "And he just doesn't know how to interact with women."

Cheyenne scoffed. "Or people."

Katrine raised an eyebrow. "You already profiled him?"

"It's my job. Don't tell me our unwanted guest doesn't remind you of that one student you had two years ago."

Katrine cringed. "Maybe just a little. But that was just a teenage boy with an infatuation."

"Teenage boys with infatuations can grow up to be men with perverse addictions."

"I'm sure it'll be fine," Katrine said. "Didn't I hear Rico say this was his last night?"

"And your point?" Cheyenne said.

Katrine sighed. "Don't get worked up over a guy who's going to be gone tomorrow."

"Fine," Cheyenne said. "I'll be outside, getting ready or something."

Cheyenne exited the tent and took a seat at the picnic table. She pulled out her cell phone. Thumbing through her contacts, she mocked Katrine's advice, "Don't get worked up." She rolled her eyes, then found her father's number and dialed. On the third ring, he picked up.

"Cheyenne," her father said. "How's the new campground?"

"It's fine," Cheyenne said.

"Doesn't sound fine," her father said. "Are you and Katrine, okay?"

She sensed where her father was going with this and attempted to redirect the conversation. "No. I mean, yes. We're fine. It's just... There's this guy next to us giving off weird vibes."

She waited for her father to respond. When he didn't, she continued. "I mean, he's definitely socially awkward, and he was checking out Katrine."

"She is a beautiful woman," her father said. "You both are. Listen, a lot of guys have sat in the back seat of my cruiser over the years. I've heard and seen it all. Men check women out all the time. He's probably in his tent rubbing one out while thinking about you two."

"Gross," Cheyenne said.

"But, true," her father said. "And if that helps to make you even more uncomfortable, good. Move campsites. Hell, you should probably move campgrounds. But, please, get out. Even with Katrine's .38, you can never be too cautious."

The tent's flap flipped open, and Katrine stepped out. She wore form-fitting jeans, a baseball cap, and a t-shirt. She also wore hiking boots and dangled a similar pair for Cheyenne in front of her.

"Who're you talking to?" Katrine asked.

Cheyenne held up a hand to silence her. Speaking into her phone, she said, "Thanks, Dad."

"I love you, kiddo," her father said. "Give my love to Katrine and tell her what I said about this guy."

"I will," Cheyenne said. "Love you, too." She hung up the phone.

Katrine settled down next to her on the bench. "Cheyenne, did you call your father?"

"He gives you his love," Cheyenne said. "What's with the boots?"

"Let me guess," Katrine said. "You told him about Rico, and he said we should move campsites."

Cheyenne nodded. "He also said Rico is probably rubbing one—"

"Ah!" Katrine said, covering her ears. "Don't want to hear it. Still, your father does make a good point."

Cheyenne's eyes lit up. "So, we're packing up?"

Katrine scooted closer to Cheyenne and lifted her chin. "Yes, love."

Cheyenne parted her lips and received Katrine's. They lingered, fully absorbed in the kiss.

Abruptly, Katrine stood. "But after we go on a hike. I hear this place has awesome trails."

"You suck," Cheyenne grumbled.

"And you like it."

Cheyenne laughed at Katrine's verbal volley, though it didn't do much to relieve her fears. She kicked off her sneakers and slipped into her hiking shoes. A part of her wished she, like Katrine, had changed outfits. Baggier clothes weren't suited for a hike. Still, she preferred not to be the subject of Rico's fantasies while she changed inside the tent.

RICO ACHED WITH LONGING as he watched the women walk, hand-in-hand, up the road. The younger woman hadn't given her name earlier, but now he allowed it to play on his tongue and lips, voicing it quietly at first.

"Cheyenne," he whispered. "Sweet Cheyenne."

When he had left Cheyenne, he had circled back around where he had hidden in the tree line behind the women's campsite. He overheard enough to know that Katrine had been partially naked, and that they were wrong about him. Though he wasn't "rubbing one out," as Cheyenne had said, he found both women deliciously attractive. He imagined the women inside their tent and rode this fantasy out until his groin bulged and his lips glistened with saliva.

He watched the women as they disappeared around a bend in the road. Then he wiped the back of his hand over his mouth and ventured into their campsite. Unlike his site, everything spoke of a feminine touch, complete with a floral print tablecloth and a matching sunshade. He crossed to the tent and caressed the outside wall where it had bulged slightly with Katrine's form. He allowed his hand to pass over the tent as he approached the flap. He toyed with the flap in gentle foreplay with his fore and middle fingers.

God, they were beautiful.

He imagined caressing the curves beneath Cheyenne's baggy clothing and running his hands down her belly. He'd start with her first. Of that, he was sure. His hand came to the cool metal of the zipper on the tent flap. He gripped it loosely, pulling it down gently. That's how he'd do it, slow and gentle, as with the others.

He paused, and his ears perked to rustling from just beyond the tree line. He stepped away from the tent. Though hours of daylight remained, he struggled to peer through the forest beyond.

"Show yourself!" Rico called out.

Dry wood cracked, and leaves rustled under someone's heavy footsteps.

"You better leave these women alone," Rico called out. "You hear me?"

The footsteps halted, and the setting sun glinted off a pair of eyes, disappearing into the shadows. Rico squinted and took a few paces toward the forest, where a dark, shapeless form staggered in the shadows. Rico didn't like someone encroaching on the territory he'd already claimed for himself. He didn't know when the women would return, but he had to protect his find.

He darted through the trees with a guttural scream and barreled into a fleshy, screeching mass. Tree branches snapped, and the forest shuddered with a cacophony of primordial and human howls that ended in a heavy thud.

CHEYENNE AND KATRINE hiked for over an hour before they returned to their campsite.

"So, we can go now, right?" Cheyenne asked.

"I suppose," Katrine said. "But admit it, this is one of the more beautiful campgrounds we've been to."

"It is," Cheyenne said. "Despite our creepy neighbor, I'm glad we made it a stop on our travels."

"You betcha, love," Katrine said, wrapping her arm around Cheyenne's waist.

"Hold up!" Cheyenne said. "Rico's site is cleared out."

Katrine gave Cheyenne a slight hip bump. "Does that mean you want to stay?"

Cheyenne crossed over to Rico's abandoned campsite. She took a few cautious steps toward the fire ring, knelt, and extended her hand over the dying embers.

"He didn't even bother to put out the fire," Cheyenne said.

Katrine pulled the cooler out of the Jeep. "Maybe you scared him off, and he left in a hurry."

"I doubt it," Cheyenne said and stood. She wanted to stay, but she thought about her father's words. "Dad did urge us to leave the campground."

Cheyenne trudged back to the campsite to find Katrine laying out bread, deli meat, and fresh vegetables.

"Katrine, didn't you hear me?" Cheyenne asked.

"I heard you, love," Katrine said. She stopped her preparations. "But that's when Rico was still next door. He isn't anymore."

Cheyenne bit her lower lip. "But—"

"You know I can't resist that look," Katrine said. She sighed. "Listen, let's eat, then we'll head over to that bar Rico mentioned. We'll get stupid drunk, then come back here and have—"

"Wild sex?" Cheyenne smirked.

Katrine grinned. "I was going to say a bonfire, but we can have that, too."

THE JEEP'S HEADLIGHTS bore down on a dive bar half a mile from the campground. Country music blared, and locals milled about outside drinking.

"Classy," Cheyenne muttered. "You've got the .38, right?"

Katrine patted the bulge of her sidearm beneath the hoodie she wore. "For the hundredth time, yes. Stop being such a worry-wort."

Cheyenne rolled her eyes. "Alright, but you're buying."

When they climbed out of the Jeep, Cheyenne's ears burned to the tune of rude catcalls.

"Moon's out," a man called. "And it's a beauty."

"You know what won't be out?" Katrine said. "Your face when I rearrange it."

The man looked away, seeking support from his buddies, who were already too drunk to be of use. Cheyenne locked her arm in Katrine's, and they headed inside the bar.

"Creeps," Cheyenne said under her breath. "I'm thinking we get a growler and leave."

Katrine raised an eyebrow. "You think this place serves growlers?"

She was right, of course. Cheyenne glanced at the bar where a red-headed woman wearing a halter-top served cheap liquor to flannel-clad men and women dressed in cowboy boots and cut-off jeans. The best they served on tap was an Irish Red, bottled and distributed by an American beer company.

Under the scrutiny of several onlookers, the couple claimed bar stools closest to the door should they need to make a quick break.

Cheyenne turned to Katrine. "About getting liquored up—"

"I know," Katrine cut her off. "We'll have one or two, then head back to the campsite."

The redhead's hips swayed as she approached from behind the bar. "Hey, girls!" she said with smiling green eyes. "What can I get ya?"

"Jack and Coke," Cheyenne said.

Katrine nudged her. "Starting strong, huh? I guess I'll have the same."

"Anything else?" The redhead asked. "You'll love the house chips."

"Sure," Cheyenne said. "We'll have that."

When the redhead walked away, Katrine put an arm around Cheyenne and kissed her. "You have as much as you want, love. I'll just get one."

"If you're planning something," Cheyenne winked. "You know you don't need liquor for that."

The redhead returned, placing the drinks in front of the women. She leaned in. "Okay. Don't take offense or anything, but I gotta ask because you two are just too cute together."

"We're married," Cheyenne and Katrine said in unison.

The redhead looked back in an apparent exchange with her male counterpart behind the bar. He nodded knowingly. She winked, then turned to the women and grinned. "Kyle had a bet. He lost. I'm Chloe. Anything else ya'll need, just give me a holler."

Cheyenne gazed at Chloe as she walked away. Katrine slapped her lightly on the arm. "I saw that."

Cheyenne shrugged. "And you didn't?" She downed her drink and immediately signaled for another.

Katrine took a sip of her drink and chuckled. "You're wasting no time."

"It's been a night," Cheyenne said.

"You got that right," Katrine added.

Chloe returned with two Jack and Cokes and the chips. "So, you two have an admirer who wants to pay for the next round." She winked. "Take it where you can get it, right?"

Cheyenne spotted the back of long, greasy, dark hair. "Shit! I can't believe Rico followed us."

"Tell him we don't accept," Katrine said and stood up.

Cheyenne grabbed the back pocket of Katrine's jeans. "Babe, it's best we get out of here without making a scene." Cheyenne turned to Chloe. "Can you tell him we're flattered by the gesture, but we're not interested?"

"I'll tell him something like that," Chloe said, then did an about-face and spoke with Kyle.

Katrine stood and pulled a few bills out of her wallet. "How about we pay up and get out of here."

Cheyenne shook as she stood. "Good idea."

Katrine wrapped an arm around Cheyenne. As they turned to leave, Cheyenne caught the profile of the patron who had bought them drinks. She gasped. "It isn't him."

The patron's features were sharp and clear, while Rico's were scarred and deep-set. The man handed Kyle a few bills, then glanced in Cheyenne's and Katrine's direction and offered them a slight wave. Exiting the bar, he kept his eyes keenly on the floor as he passed by the women.

Cheyenne forced a laugh and sat. "Might as well finish these." She grabbed one of the drinks and downed half as Katrine sat beside her.

Soon, Cheyenne's attention was taken up solely by Katrine's ramblings about a much more remote campground several hundred miles up the road. However, Cheyenne still couldn't shake the sudden exit of their unwanted admirer. One encounter with a weirdo would've been enough, but two in one day was more than she could handle. She played with the chips, shifting them around to make it look like she'd eaten something while letting the ice in the rest of her drink dissolve without taking another sip.

"Babe," Cheyenne said, cutting Katrine off. "It's getting late. I want to head back."

"Oh," Katrine said. "For a bonfire or a little snuggle time?"

"Both sound good," Cheyenne said.

"Alright, love," Katrine said and downed the rest of her drink. She called Chloe over and handed her some cash. "Keep it, you know, for taking care of us tonight."

CHEYENNE SNUGGLED NEXT to Katrine as flames danced before her.

"Are you asleep, love?" Katrine asked, caressing Cheyenne's smooth, soft skin.

Cheyenne cooed. "Enjoying the company and the quiet of the night."

Katrine shifted upright, causing Cheyenne to do the same.

"What is it, babe?" Cheyenne asked.

Katrine stood and pulled out the .38. She popped the cylinder and eyed the chambers. In the glow of the fire, Katrine's jawline clenched. Locking the gun back in place, Katrine switched off the safety. She turned, placing herself between Cheyenne and the tree line.

Cheyenne stood. "Did you hear something?"

Katrine spun to face her. "It's what I didn't hear."

Though Cheyenne wanted to crack a joke at the almost cliché way that came out, she knew better. Katrine's eyes reflected the bonfire's glow, creating an eerie intensity in her that Cheyenne had never seen.

"You're freaking me out," Cheyenne said. "There's nothing—"

The fire popped and sizzled, and Cheyenne shrieked.

Katrine wrapped her free arm around her, pulling her tight. "Someone's watching us," she said. "Love, get the Jeep started while I cover you."

Cheyenne nodded, knowing better than to question Katrine even though her head seemed to spin with a thousand questions.

Katrine planted a kiss on Cheyenne's lips, then pushed her away. "Go! I'll be right behind you."

While Katrine turned and aimed her gun into the darkness, Cheyenne bolted toward the Jeep and popped it open. She scrambled into the driver's seat and grabbed the phone they kept in the console. It took her several attempts to dial 9-1-1.

"Get the fuck back," Katrine shouted from somewhere behind the Jeep.

An operator picked up the other end of the call. Over the usual greeting, Cheyenne blurted out. "Help! Someone's in the forest and—"

Several rounds of gunfire accompanied by inhuman shrieking pierced through the night.

"Ma'am, are you safe?" The operator asked.

Another volley of gunfire rang out, followed by Katrine's scream. Tears welled up in Cheyenne's eyes, and she dropped her phone. Cheyenne wiped a sleeve across her eyes and listened to the forest's silence while the phone buzzed somewhere in the darkness of the Jeep's floor. She couldn't take the silence anymore. Katrine was out there alone and injured, or worse. She reached for the door handle. As she did, she caught movement through the rearview mirror. A figure approached. She grabbed the keys, intent on running over their assailant. The keys slipped out of her hands and onto the floor.

Cheyenne cursed and bent down. Her hand passed over the phone she had dropped, finding comfort in the rigid plastic. She grabbed the keys with a jingle and rose, stuffing the key into the ignition and turning. The engine roared to life. A tapping at the driver-side window caused her to jump and turn. Katrine gazed back at her.

"Babe," Cheyenne said, her whole being flooding with relief. "What happened out there?"

Slick, snakelike movement whipped out from Katrine, shattering the glass and sinking the end of a tentacle into Cheyenne's temple.

Pressure wrapped around Cheyenne's brain with euphoric pain. As Cheyenne's eyes rolled into the back of her head, her lover's face transformed from Katrine's to Rico's, then to her own face.

"Oh," Cheyenne moaned. Her body pulsated as blood and tears formed in the corner of her eyes. Another snakelike tentacle sank into the other side of her head and yanked her limp body out the window.

UNDER THE RISING SUN, the orange Jeep Wrangler bounced over a pothole. The driver cursed. "Primitive."

Next to her, a phone rang. She glanced at it. The word *Dad* blinked on the phone's LCD screen. She snatched up the phone.

"Dad!" Her voice croaked.

"Cheyenne?" the man asked. "Are you okay?"

She cleared her throat. "Yeah. I'm okay. Why do you ask?"

"Your voice sounds a little raw this morning," the man said.

"Must've been," she paused for a moment. "The wild sex."

"That's... okay!"

Though the man chuckled, something about it seemed inauthentic. She'd misjudged the primitive relationship between father and daughter. In the future, she'll have to be more careful. Shifts could be tricky, and the recent memories always lacked clarity.

She broke the silence. "Katrine and I are headed back."

"Great!" the man said. "We'll be—"

"Mom'll make a sumptuous dinner."

"She always does," the man said. "Cheyenne?"

"Yes?" she asked.

"You sound tired. Get some rest," the man said. "You're not quite yourself right now."

The phone went dead, and the driver tossed it beside her. She eased on the gas, propelling the Jeep forward. Though she'd already satisfied her hunger, she knew she'd need to feed again.

Tainted Summer

SUNLIGHT bore down upon Benny's closed eyelids. Waves lapped upon the shoreline, splattering saltwater against Benny's naked, sand-covered, athletic torso and calves.

He wore only his floral-patterned swim trunks. As he groaned and stretched, the sand grated against his bare back. Rising to a seated position, a burst of pain struck Benny around the back and front of his head.

"Gah!"

He squinted and rubbed his eyes. Blinking rapidly, he grew accustomed to the morning light of dawn.

"Ginger?" Benny called out to his long-time girlfriend.

Last night, he recalled, a beach crowded with countless twenty-somethings gyrating to the steady *thunk-a-thunk-a-thunk-a* of generic dance music. Ginger wore a yellow bikini top, and a matching sarong wrapped around her waist. At some point, someone handed Benny and Ginger drinks. At another point, he and Ginger danced in the center of a circle of half-naked, sweaty bodies. Similar blurred images of last night's party lapped against the shores of Benny's memory, then receded like the tide.

He called out her name again, and the whooshing of waves and squawking of seagulls answered him.

As he stood, another flash of pain struck Benny's head. Gritting his teeth, he massaged his temples. Though he lived in Beachside, South Carolina, all his life, he didn't recognize this part of the beach. The grass waving in the breeze made these shores seem incredibly remote. So did the dark, muddy waters in which the clumps of grass clung as the tide threatened to wash the shoreline away.

Benny rose and searched the beach for a lost cell phone, t-shirt, and shoes. At some point, the rising sun would burn. He needed to return to the civilization he had known all his life. That would prove difficult — if not impossible — if he didn't find a familiar landmark or his cell phone soon. While searching the beach and the shoreline, he spotted a shock of yellow clinging to the tall grass and flapping in the wind. Benny stumbled toward it, plucked it up, and brushed off the wet sand.

A torrent of realization churned in his stomach: he held Ginger's sarong. Gritting back the pain in his head, Benny swiveled on his heels and swallowed back the bile that caught in his throat. Seagulls soared above him, and seagrass swished in the breeze as Benny doubled over and heaved. When he had finished, he rose to his feet and found himself alone.

With Ginger and last night's party gone, a thousand questions ran through his head. All centered on when he and Ginger separated and how he got here.

Was it before or after they had drinks? If after, then they were drugged. If before the party, then the undercurrent of drunken strangers had forced them apart. Did they regroup later? Benny didn't have the slightest recollection. He only became aware of the party's fading ecstasy in his awakening alone on the beach. Benny wondered if Ginger was experiencing a similar awakening. He had to find her.

Stuffing the sarong into his pocket, Benny took off, hoping he headed toward home. He clung to the idea that Ginger lay asleep in her bed. If so, she'd have a good reason for leaving him behind. It didn't matter right now. There'd be time later to figure out how they separated and why she had left him stranded in only his swimming trunks.

OUT of breath, Benny came to a two-lane highway. Traffic flowed steadily, ten to fifteen car lengths between each other—enough space to dart across the road if needed.

Bending over and placing his hands on his knees, he took a moment to catch his breath. The mile marker across the road prompted a memory. He had driven the Passat while Ginger sang off-key to Blind Melon. Her hair danced in the wind, and she laughed. He needed to hear her laughter again. He needed to press on even though the bottom of his feet stung.

Route 17 ran east and west, placing him seventeen and a half miles from Beachside. He had to walk or hitchhike home.

When Benny spotted a break in traffic, he ran across the road. A car horn blared behind him as he crossed over the rumble strips. Another vehicle zipped by, and Benny caught the tail-end of expletives shouted out the window.

Turning, Benny pointed his thumb east and waited. Cars and trucks continued by, but no one stopped.

Maybe it's for the best. Who'd be dumb enough to pick up a teenager covered in sand and wearing nothing but his swim shorts?

Benny dropped his hand and began his long trek toward home. Soon, he came to mile marker sixteen, and the exposed flesh of his neck and back began to burn. By mile fifteen, thirst began to overtake him. He licked his chapped lips, pulling away a layer of flaking skin in the process.

Behind him, a siren whooped once, and lights flashed. A sheriff's cruiser crawled past and pulled over.

A deputy stepped out of the vehicle and waited, one hand on the grip of his sidearm. Benny approached the deputy, who held up a hand.

"That's close enough, son," the deputy said. "I'm Deputy Hicks. What brings you out here?"

"I was at a ... I don't know," Benny croaked.

"That's alright," Hicks said. "Do you have any I.D.?"

"No. But I'm Benny Strickland. John Stickland's kid."

The deputy gripped his sidearm tighter. "You're not under arrest or anything, but I'm going to need you to place your hands on the trunk of my cruiser and spread your legs. You understand?"

Nodding, Benny complied.

"You got anything on you that will poke or stab me?"

"In my trunks?!" Benny said, wondering whether the deputy was purposefully missing the obvious—he couldn't possibly hide anything.

Deputy Hicks didn't comment on Benny's sarcastic remark. Instead, he patted Benny down and turned out one empty pocket. When he stuck his hand in the other pocket, he pulled out the yellow sarong.

"Stand up and face me," Hicks instructed.

Benny faced the officer's scrutinizing gaze.

Hicks held up the sarong. "You mind telling me where you got this?"

"It's my girlfriend's," Benny said.

"Hand's back on the trunk. I'm placing you under arrest."

Too tired to struggle or protest, Benny allowed himself to be cuffed and guided into the back of the cruiser.

As he sat back against his cuffed hands, Benny made one request. "I'm really thirsty. Do you have any water?"

"Hold on a sec," Hicks said as he closed the door. The cruiser's trunk popped open, and a moment later, Hicks opened the passenger door and tilted the water bottle toward Benny's mouth.

"Drink slowly. You've been missing for days."

Days?

Benny sipped and gulped. Hicks removed the bottle, screwed the top back on, and shut the door.

The driver's side door opened, and Hicks took his seat and strapped in. A moment later, Benny gazed out the window as the beach landscape passed.

"I was gone for days?"

"That's right. Your parents reported you missing, and a BOLO was released," Deputy Hicks said. "Where'd you and Ginger Larson go off to?"

"A party. But that was just last night."

Hicks eyed him with a raised eyebrow through the rearview mirror. "Maybe it'll come to you in interrogation."

Benny doubted it. "Where's Ginger?"

"Still missing," Hicks said.

The cruiser stopped at Beachside Precinct, a two-story brick structure crammed between a bakery and a surf shop. Once inside, Hicks uncuffed Benny and instructed him to take a seat.

"Your parents have been notified. They'll be along shortly with a change of clothes. In the meantime, what can you remember about the last few days?"

"First of all. There is no way I've been on that beach for days."

Hicks pulled out a notebook and pen. "Is this the beach where you had the party or another one?"

"Another one. I didn't recognize it." Benny told him about waking up with a headache and finding his way to the road.

Jotting down a note into his pad, Hicks nodded. "What else can you remember?"

"Do you want me to start at the party? Or before then?"

"Whichever one you think will help."

Benny's eyes widened. "I remember now. There was this guy named Gary Barlow. He wore a Stetson hat. He's the one who invited us to the party. No. He invited Ginger. I just ... uh ... "

"Wasn't invited?" Hicks asked. "But you came along anyway?"

"Something like that," Benny furrowed his brow. "Can I get a drink of water and some Advil? My head is still killing me."

Hicks sighed and got up. "Why not?"

Benny began his story as the deputy returned with the requested water and painkiller. "Yesterday—or a few days ago—I was at work..."

BENNY gazed out the window of Beachside Cafe, a grin spreading across his face at the sight of the crashing waves. The sunny skies and summer breeze promised a perfect morning for surfing, just as his weather app had predicted.

"Are ya gonna gawk out the window or bus tables?" Mr. Lowery's voice broke Benny's reverie. Benny turned to see his boss glaring, a toothpick clenched between his teeth.

Blushing, Benny busied himself with clearing the rest of the table and wiping it down. Still, he couldn't help but steal another look out the window, especially as Ginger walked through the door, an apron over her shoulder.

"How's, uh?" Ginger nodded toward Mr. Lowery.

Benny shrugged. "Same as always."

"Rush hour in five," Mr. Lowery called out.

Ginger rolled her eyes. "That's my cue," she said, slipping on her apron and disappearing behind the counter.

A moment later, Beachside Cafe bustled with breakfast—the best and only meal this establishment served. Sometime mid-shift, a well-dressed man wearing a dark Stetson walked in and took the first open seat at the counter.

With a radiant smile, Ginger approached the man from behind the counter. He said something to Ginger, who touched her hand to her chest and laughed. Benny grinned, having seen her do this a thousand times with absolute strangers while taking their orders. Politeness, even the right flirtation, always generated a larger tip.

They exchanged a few more words until Ginger caught Benny's gaze and blushed. She turned her back on the man for a moment as she filled a mug with coffee, just long enough for the man to look over his shoulder and give Benny a nod. Benny averted his attention back to clearing and washing tables.

As the morning passed by, the man remained at the counter, sipping the same coffee and watching people. At the time, Benny didn't think much about it. Plenty of people passed through town daily, some of whom he never saw again. Others, like this man, have strange behaviors or are looking to "get away." Beachside, a tiny resort town, saw all kinds. A man who never once took off his Stetson fit into the "all kinds" category.

At the end of their shift, Benny and Ginger met outside the cafe.

"Ready to hit the waves?" Benny asked.

"For sure!" Ginger said. "We've also been invited to a party tonight."

"Tonight? Whose party?"

"Gary invited us." She handed Benny a black, glossy card with white lettering.

Gary Barlow
Your party is my business.

"Stetson guy?" Benny shrugged. "I've never heard of him."

Ginger's eyes sparkled. "He's from L.A."

Knowing she'd go without him anyway, Benny agreed.

Benny and Ginger parted ways after a light lunch at his house. She went to her parents' house, and he went to his bedroom. After changing into wetsuits and grabbing their boards, they joined others hanging out on the beach or catching the perfect waves.

Benny paddled out, sat on his board, and watched as a promising wave approached. Meanwhile, Ginger paddled toward a rising crest and hooted as she rose with the swell.

Benny laughed, but his laughter soon turned into a frown when he spotted a figure wearing a Stetson hat on the shoreline.

Ginger's wave died down, and she toppled off her board. Climbing back on, she paddled toward Benny.

"Why the frown?"

Benny looked again, and the man was gone. "I thought I saw that Gary guy."

She followed his gaze. "Nope! Another wave's coming. Your turn."

"You go ahead," Benny said.

"Your loss." Ginger paddled off.

Though Benny eventually caught a few waves, the lurking sense of being watched distracted him, causing him to wipe out several times.

As they called it quits for the day and headed home, Benny couldn't shake the feeling that something wasn't right about Gary Barlow and his invitation to the party. But with Ginger by his side, he pushed aside those doubts and focused on enjoying the rest of the day.

DEPUTY Hicks scribbled down a few notes while Benny sipped from a glass of water.

"This business card," Hick's began. "Do you know where you or Ginger left it?"

"I don't remember who had it last. It might be in my room on the dresser," Benny said. He downed the last of the water and held it up. "Do you mind?"

Hicks stood and took the glass back to the sink. Meanwhile, Benny rubbed his temples. He tried to picture the business card. Hicks returned and set the glass down. Benny reached out and grasped it but didn't pick it up.

"I don't think the business card will be useful," Benny said. "I don't remember seeing a phone number on it."

Hicks nodded. "We'll look into it."

The front door of the precinct opened. Benny's parents, John and Elise Strickland, entered. Their faces were strained with worry lines, and their eyes revealed relief.

Benny stood. "What took you so long?"

"We got here as soon as possible," his father said.

Benny's mother closed the distance between Benny and herself. She embraced him.

"We're just glad to see you're alright."

Benny's father turned toward the deputy. "Hicks! Where's Sheriff Kinsley?"

Deputy Hicks stood. "Out of town until next week. As the most senior —"

"You wouldn't be questioning my boy without his lawyer present," Benny's father said.

Deputy Hicks shifted his weight from one foot to another. "No, Mr. Strickland! What information Benny provided, he did so voluntarily."

"Consider the interview over then," John Strickland said. He turned toward Benny and his mother. "We brought you a change of clothes. I'm sure the good deputy will accommodate a private place to change."

"That'll be fine," Hicks said.

Mrs. Stickland handed Benny a bag. "Do you need anything else? Food?"

"I could eat," Benny said, though he didn't feel particularly hungry.

Hicks huffed and held out a hand. "I'd like to inspect the bag."

Benny handed the bag to Hicks, who made a show of pulling out each item and shaking it out, then wading the items up and stuffing them back into the bag.

"Follow me," Hicks said and handed the bag to Benny.

Benny and his parents followed Hicks around a corner past two cells. An unkempt middle-aged man sat on a bench in one of the cells. No one occupied the other.

The keys on Hicks' belt loop jingled as he unclipped them and unlocked the unoccupied cell. The door creaked as it swung open while Benny's heart thumped rapidly.

John Strickland cleared his throat. "I'm sure, deputy, you have a bathroom Benny can use instead."

"Of course," Hicks said and clipped the keys onto the belt loop. "It's just down the hall. Follow me."

Benny faced his parents. "You guys don't think I had something to do with Ginger's disappearance, do you?"

His mother averted her eyes to the floor while his father's jaw muscles tightened. That's all he needed to know. They had doubts.

Benny followed Hicks down the hallway. Once in the bathroom, the deputy unlocked the door and motioned for Benny to enter.

"Don't try to go anywhere," Hicks said. "We'll be just down the hall past those cells."

"Thanks for looking out, I guess," Benny said as he entered.

Once he locked the door, Benny opened the bag his parents brought him: a t-shirt, underwear, cut-off jean shorts, and slip-on checkered sneakers. Stripping naked, he longed for a warm shower as he did his best to brush the grit off his body. Benny slipped on the shorts and felt the right front pocket bunch up. Stuffing his hand in, he grabbed a small wad of cash. He flattened out each bill and counted—a couple of fives, three ones, and two tens. He glanced at the frosted window of the bathroom and smirked.

Escape hadn't crossed his mind until he discovered the loose bills he'd left in his favorite shorts before the last washing. He doubted his mother would've snuck the money in the pocket. His father, a small-town real estate lawyer, and his mother, his assistant, would advise him to stay put. Running, they would tell him, would only make him look guilty.

But guilty of what? My girlfriend running off at a party? Waking up alone on a beach only to learn three days of his life had completely disappeared?

This was all a waste of time, Benny realized. Deputy Hicks should be out looking for Ginger, and his parents should be talking with her parents to organize a search party or something. If they were going to waste their time on him, then he'd have to take action.

Benny unlocked the bathroom window and opened it to reveal black iron bars. He let out a sigh. "Dammit!"

A knock came at the door. "Son. Are you just about ready?"

"Be there in a sec, Dad!" He closed and locked the window. Benny opened the bathroom door.

His father offered him a slight smile. "You're looking a little more human. Deputy Hicks says you're due back sometime tomorrow. But before then, you'll tell me everything you remember."

BENNY brooded in the backseat of his father's BMW i7. The night he drove Ginger in his VW Passat, she hadn't given him an address to the party. Instead, she had read him directions to the beach where the party had been held.

Benny sat forward. "Dad! Where's the Passat?"

Mr. Strickland glanced at his son, then at his wife. "Still missing. Why do you ask?"

"I don't exactly remember where the party was held, but the GPS tracker on the car—"

"I know where you're going with this, but it'll have to wait."

They pulled into the driveway next to his mom's white Prius.

Ginger's parents rose from the front porch. George Larson glared at Benny as they approached while Diane Larson wrung her hands. Benny once again wanted to escape.

"Benny," John said. "Wait here. I'll take care of this."

John Strickland stepped out of the car and slammed the door shut. He approached Ginger's father and blocked his path.

"I should get out there," Benny said. He reached for the door.

"Don't," Mrs. Strickland said. "Getting in the way will only make things worse. Let your father handle this. That's his job."

Benny gritted his teeth and sighed. From his vantage point, he realized his mother was right. All he could do was watch.

"Get out of my way, John," George Larson yelled. "I intend to find out what your boy did to our daughter."

"Benny's been missing for three days. What do you think he knows?"

Mr. Larson threw his hands into the air. "I don't know John! More than we do. For all we know, he killed her and dumped her body somewhere."

Before John Strickland could respond, Mrs. Larson released a pent-up cry.

"Diane!" George Larson shouted. "Will you knock that off?"

"I get it, George," John said. "You're upset. We both are. But now isn't the time. The police are doing their part. Let me do mine. If anything turns up, I'll call you."

Mr. Larson locked eyes with Benny. With a reddened face, he pointed at Benny. Benny's heart rate quickened as he saw his father shift his stance, thus blocking Mr. Strickland's sight. A moment later, Mr. Larson turned and guided his sobbing wife away.

As Ginger's parents walked away, Mr. Larson put an arm around his wife. "One way or the other, Diane. We'll make sure there's justice for Ginger."

Benny's father turned. "It's over for now. Let's go inside and see if we can sort this out."

Following his mother out of the car, Benny trudged past his father and into the house.

Benny plopped on the sofa while his father closed and locked the front door.

"John," Mrs. Strickland said. "Why don't I get our son something to eat before you cross-examine him."

"It's okay, Mom," Benny said. "I'm not really hungry."

"There," Mr. Strickland sat. "He's not hungry. Shall we start with why? It's like you've already eaten."

Benny glanced at his mother and scuffed the bottom of his foot on the floor. "That's just it. I can't explain it. Maybe they fed us while I was held captive."

Benny's parents exchanged a glance.

"You guys don't believe me. I swear I told Deputy Hick's everything I could remember. After showing up to the party, my memory is still kinda fuzzy."

"Did you tell him about the GPS tracker on your car?" Mrs. Stickland asked.

"No, that just came to me."

Mr. Stickland nodded. "Elise, let's hear what Benny has to say. Benny, why don't you tell us everything you told Office Hicks?"

As with Hicks, Benny began his story with his shift at the diner and ended it with Ginger showing him the card she got from Gary Barlow. "I'm not sure, but I think the card is upstairs in my room."

Mr. Stickland nodded. "Tell me about your idea with the GPS tracker."

"That's the thing," Benny said. "Ginger didn't have an address. I think she used GPS coordinates given to her on her phone. I just drove while she gave me directions. It was dark, and the roads were winding. I don't think I could get back to the spot if I tried."

"Ginger's parents already contacted the cell phone carrier. Her last known location was twenty miles off the coast. I'll see if they can access her messages or notes on the cloud."

While Benny's mother took notes, his father continued. "What about this party?"

Placing his head in his hands, Benny shifted in his seat and rested his elbows on his thighs. He rubbed his temples and squinted. An image of Ginger dressed in her bikini came to mind. She smiled at him and laughed playfully while the dance music thumped. Ginger took his hand while she raised a plastic cup to her lips. Benny swiped a cup from a tray and drank.

"It was dark," Benny said. "Drinks were given out. Something bitter."

"Cocktails, likely," his mother offered.

"Stupid," his father added. "When you're at a party, never drink from a container you didn't open yourself."

"Thanks, Dad," Benny said.

"Was this Barlowe character there?" Mr. Stickland asked.

"Gary?" Benny shook his head. "I never even met him except for that one time. Honestly, I think he was targeting Ginger."

Benny's father stood. "We'll see if Hicks ever checked the security footage outside of Beachside Cafe. Benny, head on upstairs and see if you can find that card, then get some rest. We'll relay all this information to the sheriff's office."

Benny looked at his mother. "Can I get a sandwich or something?"

She exchanged a glance with her husband before replying. "I'll bring something up in a bit."

As Benny headed up the steps, he couldn't help but wonder about the last interaction between his mother and father. Did they believe him? He didn't think so but was determined to prove his innocence. He had nothing to do with Ginger's disappearance except going to the party with her. Still, what were Gary's intentions?

Benny found his room tidied up, a far cry from the rumpled mess he had left three nights ago before he and Ginger headed out. His mother must've busied herself cleaning up, which changed everything. The card could be anywhere. He started with the most logical places—under the bed and behind the desk or dresser. When these turned up short, Benny pulled out a dresser drawer and began rummaging through pockets.

A knock came at the door.

"It's open," Benny called.

His mother greeted him with a smile and offered him a glass of water and a sandwich on a small plate.

"Thanks, Mom," Benny said as he took the plate. "I was looking for that little black business card."

"No luck? I didn't see it when I straightened up your room," his mother said.

"You went through my stuff?" Benny asked.

"Once the sheriff's office was contacted, I didn't have much else to do," his mother said. "How're you doing?"

Benny shrugged. "I'm fine. Just want to be left alone."

"Are you sure?" his mother said, peeking beyond Benny and into the room.

"Good night, Mom."

After a brief hesitation, Mrs. Stickland turned and walked away. Benny listened for his mother's receding footsteps before setting the sandwich and glass of water on the desk. He wondered if his parents had found the card. If they did, they had no reason to hold out on him. Besides, his father would've turned to anything that would've helped in finding him. More than likely, he or Ginger had dropped the card at the party or left it in the Passat. In either case, he'd have to do some digging.

After powering up the computer, he shut and locked the bedroom door. Returning to the desk, he sat, bit into the sandwich, and logged in.

As he chewed, he opened a web browser. He searched for Gary *Barlow, Party Planner, Your Party is My Business, Los Angeles.*

Several Gary Barlows and various party planners in the L.A. area popped up. He clicked the images tab and saw the faces of men he didn't recognize. Benny wondered if this guy was a ghost — someone who is only found if he wants to be found.

Benny took another bite of the sandwich and chewed slowly. Hours scouring the internet would likely prove fruitless. He had to go back to the beach. Maybe there he'd find a clue. He had to go when he knew his parents slept soundly.

RISING from a sleepless night, Benny climbed out of bed and listened. Though his father told him not to go anywhere, Benny had resolved from the moment he woke up on the beach that he would have to find Ginger.

Once dressed in dark clothing, Benny walked lightly down the steps and found the hooks where his parents kept their keys—one to the BMW and the other to the Prius. He chose the Prius, which would draw much less attention than the BMW. Grasping the keys in one hand to keep them from jingling, he unlocked the side door. Staying close to the house and using the landscaping for cover, Benny slipped around the house and onto the front driveway. He scurried over to the Prius, slid into the driver's side seat, and hit the ignition button.

"Too easy," Benny muttered as he backed the car out of the driveway while keeping his eyes locked on the house. The curtains didn't stir, and the lights didn't turn on. "Way too easy," Benny said.

He eased his foot on the gas, navigated the vehicle out of the neighborhood, and came to an intersection. A business occupied each of the four corners. Adjacent to his corner, the 7-11 prompted Benny's sense of necessity. He needed basic supplies — water, food, and a phone. 7-11 carried all three. Benny hugged the turn closely when the light turned green, causing his left tire to hop a curb. He hit the brake, took a deep breath, and eased the car into a spot. Cutting the engine, Benny reached for the door handle. Beside him, another vehicle marked *Beachside Police* pulled up.

Benny shrank in his seat as a deputy entered the 7-11. The officer, a male in his early twenties, paused inside the store and greeted the cashier. Turning his back on the parking lot, he busied himself at the coffee kiosk while occasionally looking around the store. With the officer's attention diverted, Benny exited the Prius and walked to the store's entrance. He took a deep breath and opened the door.

The officer gave Benny a slight nod as they passed each other—the officer to the cashier's counter and Benny to an aisle where he hoped he could avoid raising suspicion.

The police radio crackled, *10-31 at 102 Main Street. Please acknowledge.*

The officer answered the call and returned to his vehicle. A moment later, the siren wailed and soon faded away.

With no reason to delay and risk any exposure, Benny grabbed a few snacks and a prepaid phone. The total came to just under thirty dollars. Benny pulled out the wad of cash in his pocket and handed it to the cashier without counting or waiting for the change.

———⟊⟊⟍⟍⟠⟠———

SPEEDING down Route 17, Benny glanced in the rearview mirror. No cars meant no tails—civilian or police. He had a few hours before dawn illuminated the road. If that happened, his mom would soon knock on his bedroom door and prompt him to have breakfast before his bussing shift at Beachside Cafe. He couldn't let that happen.

Somewhere past mile marker 25, Benny came to an intersection. He hung a left. In the dark, the road struck a sense of familiarity. He and Ginger came this way a few nights ago. The next right took him through a sparsely populated neighborhood of trailer homes and RVs used as homes. Another left and two miles down the road brought Benny to a boat slip and a dock. He stopped the vehicle and gazed through the windshield.

The scene from three nights ago unfolded in Benny's mind's eye. Strings of colored lights tied to a yacht big enough for a sizable gathering. The beach hadn't been as crowded as his flashes of memory led him to believe. Maybe a hundred or so dockside and half of that in the Yacht. Not a huge party, but large enough to get lost in. Benny couldn't remember if he recognized anyone from the party or whether Gary Barlow in his Stetson had been there. Upon his arrival, someone had handed drinks to Benny and Ginger. After a few swigs, Benny allowed the party to sweep him away.

Benny flicked on the Prius's high beams, turned on the new phone, and found the flashlight app. He hoped to illuminate any shadows the car's lights cast. Stepping out of the vehicle, Benny pointed the light toward the ground. He walked, kicking up sand to unearth Barlow's business card if Ginger or he happened to have dropped it a few nights ago. His kicking turned up a used condom, hair bands, a pair of sunglasses, and several crushed cans of cheap beer. He had to be in the right place.

When he came to the dock, Benny took in the moonlight's glow off the water's surface. He took a deep breath, and the bubbling of the incoming tide below the deck caused his stomach to lurch. He realized then that he had been on the Yacht, maybe for several days. Or maybe not. He remembered a dark room and the bubbling of water. He turned away from the ocean and stepped off the dock onto dry, stable ground.

He scanned the area around the dock's entrance. He spotted a black business card with white lettering inches from his feet.

"Barlow," Benny muttered as he picked up the card and examined it.

The damp ground had softened the corners and edges of the card. But there was no mistaking that this card had been given out by Gary Barlow or one of his associates if he had any.

Benny flipped the card over, which contained ten typed numbers, followed by four handwritten numbers. He dialed the first ten.

A man's voice, deep and gruff, answered. "Invitation code."

Benny read the four handwritten numbers.

"That code has expired," the man said.

"What do you mean?" Benny asked.

No answer.

Benny asked again, only to realize the man on the other end of the phone had already hung up.

Trying again, Benny waited as the phone rang eight or nine times before the man answered.

"Listen, kid!" The man yelled. "The codes have been used, so unless you read it wrong—"

"I didn't read it wrong," Benny said. "I was at the party a few nights ago. I don't know what you guys did to me or my girlfriend—"

Deep and sinister laughter cut Benny off. "I feel for you, but there's nothing I can do. If you know what's good for you, you'll put it to rest."

"How about a meet-up?" Benny asked.

The man answered him with a long silence, then a sigh. "Okay. Meet at 104 Capeside Drive at 2 a.m. Come alone."

Benny hung up the phone without bothering to thank the man or confirm that he would be there. No need. The man meant business. His warning to let it rest told him as much. Benny returned to the car.

On the horizon before him, dawn's first light greeted Benny. Through the rearview mirror, flashing red and blue lights told Benny what he already knew: He'd been out too late. His parents must've spotted the car missing and tracked his GPS location.

When the cruiser came to a stop, Benny pulled up a pant leg and slipped the cell phone and business card into his crew-length sock. Officer Hicks stepped out of the car and marched up to the driver's side of the Prius. Benny rolled down the window.

"What the hell are you doing, son?" Hicks demanded.

"This is where the party happened," Benny said. "I remember everything."

Hicks squinted. "I'd arrest you here, but your parents followed me to this location."

Stepping away from the Prius, Hicks motioned for Benny to step out. Benny did so and turned away from the ocean. His father and mother stood on opposite sides of the BMW.

"Benny," Mr. Stickland called. "You and your mother can switch seats as we head into the precinct to sort things out."

Reluctantly, Benny agreed. With his head bowed, he passed by his mother and joined his father in the BMW.

"You've got some explaining to do," Mr. Stickland said, turning the car around.

Benny told his father everything he recalled from the party—the yacht, the beach, and the people. But he left out two crucial details—that he had found Barlowe's card with the phone number and called to set up a meeting tonight. He didn't need anyone messing up his chances of getting answers and finding Ginger.

BENNY and his father sat in a gray room with cold, hard seats and a steel table. They faced a one-way mirror beyond which Benny imagined a hardened detective with narrow, scrutinizing eyes. Benny bounced alternating legs while replaying everything he could remember about that night. Next to him, his father studied the notes he had compiled.

The interrogation door opened, and a middle-aged man with graying temples and dark eyes stepped in. Deputy Hicks followed right behind him.

"This is Special Agent David Kane," Hicks said. "He's been caught up on Benny's story."

Kane unbuttoned his sports coat and sat. He offered Benny and his father a smile and a handshake.

Benny's father returned the handshake. "What business does the FBI have in my son's case?"

"I promise you this is just a formality. Benny, Mr. Strickland," said Agent Kane. "The evidence suggests Benny and Ms. Larson are likely the victims of a human trafficking ring. We've been tracking the ring up and down the East Coast. Benny, tell us what prompted you to sneak out and head down to the docks."

Benny waited for his father's signal before answering. "My memory's coming back. I had to check it for myself."

"And you're certain that dock is where the party had been," Kane said.

"He's certain," Mr. Stickland said. "I understand there's a team searching the site for more clues."

"That's right," said Agent Kane. "Benny, we know there was a party, and you and Ginger were there. What more can you tell us?"

Benny closed his eyes and rubbed his temples. "There was this yacht. Nice, you know. Like what you'd see in movies. I think I was on board, and there were a lot of people. Maybe two hundred. Most were younger, like me and Ginger. Some were college-age."

Agent Kane flipped open a manila folder and turned it while sliding it across the table. "Do you remember seeing this man?"

Benny examined a sketch of a man with round eyes and a cunning smile. "That's Gary Barlow! But I didn't see him at the party. The last time I saw him was —"

"We know," Agent Kane said. "On the beach."

"Yes!" Benny said. "He was watching me. I am sure of it. Maybe waiting for —"

Mr. Stickland placed a hand on Benny's arm. "Stick to only what you know, son. Agent Kane, do you have any questions for Benny?"

"Do you remember any specifics on board the yacht?"

Benny recalled his father's advice to stick to only what he knew to be true. "I remember a dark room. The boat rocked. That made me seasick."

"Was Ms. Larson or anyone else in the room with you?"

The image of a dark form standing in front of a bright light washed up on the shores of Benny's memory. "Someone. A man."

"Would you be able to describe him?"

"No," Benny said. "He had a light shining directly in my face. Someone else grabbed me from behind and pulled me off the boat."

After another round of questions in which Benny repeated himself five more times, Agent Kane stood and fastened the top button of his sports coat. "Gentlemen, I think we're done for now. If Deputy Hicks has no further questions for you, you're free to go."

Upon their release, Benny sat in the passenger seat of his father's i7. He could not help but feel like they were being watched. Maybe he had seen too many crime shows, but he suspected Agent Kane had put a tail on them. Through the side mirror, he kept an eye on a black sedan a few cars behind them.

Had it been following them ever since they left the precinct?

He couldn't remember.

The sedan followed as they exited Beachside and came to the surrounding communities. If his father had noticed, he hadn't let on. Mr. Stickland's eyes narrowed and focused on the road before him, his jaws clenching and unclenching. Benny knew that look. His father was deep in thought, mentally sorting and resorting the details of Benny's story.

"Dad," Benny said. "I wish I could remember more."

Mr. Stickland navigated the car around the next corner and flicked on his four-ways. He brought the car to a stop and turned to Benny. "What aren't you telling me?"

The black sedan passed them on the left. Its tinted windows obscured the driver and any passengers inside.

"I think someone's been following us," Benny said.

"I've noticed," Mr. Stickland said. "So, I'll ask again. What aren't you telling me?"

Benny sighed and unbuckled his seatbelt. He pulled the cell phone and business card from his sock and handed them to his father.

"What's this?" Mr. Strickland asked.

"I called the numbers on the back of the card. They want to meet tonight at 2 a.m."

His father examined the card and sighed. "Do you have a location yet?"

Benny nodded. "They also told me to come alone."

"If I know what's good for me."

"Right, I'll have a few of my P.I.s check it out. In the meantime, do not mention this to your mother or the Larsons."

Benny knew better than to question his father.

UNDER the moon's light, Benny walked a half block toward 104 Capeside Drive, a two-story warehouse surrounded by cracked pavement and a rusted security fence. As he approached, Benny wondered how long the warehouse had been abandoned and whether his father's contacts would watch his every move.

Ten minutes before, Benny hadn't questioned his father when he fixed an earpiece into his own ear and another into Benny's ear. But away from his father, Benny had questions. Why would a lawyer have this kind of communication equipment?

"Benny, pick up the pace," his father said. "It's two minutes to two a.m."

Benny knew not to answer. Too many movies showed a novice like him meeting the forever sleep just because they couldn't keep their cool. Still, he couldn't help his body's involuntary reaction to fear and excitement when he stood at the main entrance to the warehouse.

He had followed instructions. Now what? Balling his fist, Benny raised his hand to knock. He didn't get a chance. Burly hands grabbed him from behind. As he cried out, coarse material was shoved over his head, shrouding him in total darkness.

Benny struggled, but the burly hands that held him tightened and pulled him into a mass of hardened muscles. Another set of hands grabbed one of Benny's wrists and zip-tied it to the other.

"Struggle, and you're done for," the recognizable gruff voice ordered into his ear.

Benny complied, and his captors spun him once or twice before leading him off. He became keenly aware of the change in terrain from rough concrete to uncut grass and soft sand. His ears perked up to the ocean's tide and his father's voice in his ear.

"You're behind the warehouse. Don't worry. My guys are following from a distance. You're doing great."

Though a bag concealed his vision, Benny still fought the urge to turn his head. He imagined men on rooftops holding sniper rifles but opted for the more realistic. Binoculars would be as effective at keeping overwatch as a scope mounted on a gun would. Still, doubt lapped at the shores of Benny's imagination. His father was just a lawyer, wasn't he?

"Watch your feet," the familiar gruffness ordered. "Steady incline on your next step."

Benny's feet landed on wooden boards that gave a little under his weight. Water gurgled below him.

His father's voice confirmed what Benny already sensed. "They are taking you onto a yacht. Hold tight."

"Step up!"

Benny recognized the gentle sway of the boat's deck. His captors guided him down a set of steps through what Benny concluded as a hallway and another set of steps.

They grabbed him and forced him to a seated position on the floor. A moment later, a door creaked shut. Benny shifted his position and felt the floor. It was textured, like wood.

He pounded a heel onto the floor. "Crap!"

"Hello?" A voice croaked. "Benny?"

Tears formed in Benny's eyes. "Ginger? Are you okay?"

"Benny? They said you jumped overboard. That you left me."

"How long ago?" Benny asked, though he knew the answer. Sometime over twenty-four hours ago. He'd woken up on the beach. Maybe he'd hit his head, or perhaps they'd been drugging him and Ginger this whole time. That would explain the loss of memory and appetite. It had been about four days.

"I don't know. They've kept me in the dark this whole time, " Ginger said, beginning to cry.

Benny shifted toward her. "I'm sorry for leaving you behind. I don't know what happened. But we're going to get out of this. Let's get closer."

He and Ginger shifted and shuffled their weight against the floor until their bodies touched side by side.

The door creaked open.

"Well, look at you two," said a man's voice, deep and resonating.

"Who are you people?" Benny demanded.

"You don't know how hard it is to pull someone out of hiding. He's been a ghost, you know.."

Benny concluded this man was their leader. "Who's been a ghost?"

"Your father," the apparent leader said.

"My father?!" Benny said. "What's he got to do with this?"

"Let's go, take both of them."

A pair of beefy hands hoisted Benny to his feet and guided him out the door.

Ginger screeched. "Watch it!"

"Where are you taking us?" Benny shouted. He struggled against the hands that held him.

"Top deck," the gruff voice chimed in.

"I know you probably want to ask ol' GB a question," said the leader with a hint of laughter. *GB*, that's what your father used to call me. Others called me Sir or Don." He paused as he reminisced. But... not Billy Boy. Nope. He always called me GB. He was my second in command. Childhood pals, if you'd like."

"GB, Sir..." Benny spoke up. "Er... Don, if I may."

"You may," GB said. "Watch your next step."

Benny's foot collided with the bottom step. His captor pulled him back, steadying him.

"Who's Billy Boy?"

They stopped. With the bag still over Benny's head, he could only imagine GB glaring at him from the top step.

The answer came directly through Benny's earpiece: *That's me, son. I'll explain later. Now do as he says, and you'll be fine.*

Then came a sharp thud. "Ouch!" Ginger screeched.

"Keep them in one piece, boys," GB said. "Let's head to the top. Then little Benny's question will be answered."

A cool evening breeze fluttered against Benny's skin. He felt Ginger's presence by his side — her warmth and steady breathing. Simultaneously, his heart raced, and not just from blindly climbing the rapid incline of two flights of steps and one spiral staircase leading to the yacht's top deck.

Benny, his father's voice spoke. *When I tell you to, duck.*

"Billy Boy!" GB called out.

Benny sensed his father was in sight but not close enough for GB to pick up on their communication through the earpiece.

GB gripped Benny's arm and shouted louder. "William Di Fonzo!"

The man behind Benny released his grip on him and growled. "That's your old man's real name. William Di Fonzo."

Fear and a sense of betrayal took over. Benny pulled away from GB, but the man's grip held fast.

"Take it easy, son." Benny's father called out from an indecipherable distance. "GB! You've found me. Now let my son and his girlfriend go."

"I don't think so, Billy Boy."

Benny grunted as the butt of a gun jammed into his side.

"See, Benny," GB said. "Your father was my top advisor, and then he ratted us out. It cost me my son; now it's gonna cost him."

"Now!" his father called out.

Benny pulled away.

THWAP.

The weight of GB's body drew Benny to the ground.

THWAP. THWAP.

Two more bodies thudded to the ground. Ginger screeched.

Strong hands lifted him up and pulled the coarse fabric off his face. His father — John Stickland or William Di Fonza? — gazed back at Benny.

"I'm sorry it went down like this."

"What! Was I bait or something?" Benny shouted.

"Turn around," his father said. "Let me cut you loose."

When the zip ties snapped loose, Benny rubbed his raw wrists.

"You have a lot of questions," his father continued.

Benny spotted Ginger being led away by a man and a woman dressed in black.

"Whatever," Benny said. "I'm going to check on Ginger."

Benny turned away from his father and climbed down to the second deck.

"Ginger!"

Ginger turned, and her escorts did the same. The woman nodded and smiled. Ginger ran toward Benny, who received her in an embrace. Benny was aware that his father watched over them from the top deck. He had been hiding this whole time, putting Benny and everyone else in danger, but from whom? He didn't want to speculate, but he knew he would do for Ginger what his father failed to do for him — keep her far from trouble.

BENNY and his father sat on the deck behind the beach house overlooking the ocean.

"Your mother knew," Benny's father said.

"Like, how much?" Benny asked. "And does this mean my last name isn't Strickland?"

His father laughed. "Of course it is. That life is behind us."

"And who's GB?"

"Gino Bagli and I knew each other as boys in the old neighborhood. Your mother grew up a few blocks away. Gino got mixed up in a money laundering scheme. I went along to watch his back. Eventually, he took out our boss. When your mother and I married, I was already too deep. Then she got pregnant with you. We needed to get out."

"How did that happen?"

"I tipped off the FBI and allowed myself to get caught in a raid at one of our warehouses. In exchange for information, Agent Kane offered us witness protection. Unfortunately, GB was already in the wind."

"So, this wasn't about sex trafficking?"

His father looked up and took a deep breath. "No. Kane used that as a cover. He didn't need the local sheriffs poking around. The interrogation was simply a rushed formality to keep Hicks in the dark. Kane suspected you'd been in contact with one of GB's associates."

Benny's eyes widened. "He was watching me that whole time."

Benny's father nodded.

The patio door behind them slid open. "Ginger's here."

Benny jumped up and grinned. "At least the entire summer isn't totally ruined."

His father gave him a half smile. "Only slightly tainted. Have fun and no —"

"Parties. I've got this dad."

Benny passed by his mother, who gave him a slight smile.

"You ready," Ginger grinned.

Benny took her hand. "Let's hit some waves.

He felt betrayed by both of his parents, and he sensed there was still more they weren't telling him. Still, he knew they were just trying to protect. He could forgive them in time, but he needed to clear his head for now.

Benny grabbed his surfboard, and he and Ginger headed to the beach.

Author's Notes

The short story—a blissful interruption amidst lives brimming with work, technology, family obligations, friends, and binge-watching.

Throughout my six years of publishing, I've encountered countless individuals who echo the same sentiment: "I would love to read, but I am just too busy!" Trust me, I understand this excuse all too well. It's undeniable that life gets hectic, yet it's equally undeniable that we often fill our time with less fulfilling pursuits—mindless scrolling or rewatching decades-old TV series for the umpteenth time.

In the midst of this chaos, what we truly need is not another excuse to forego literature, but rather the willingness to set aside these distractions and indulge, even if only for a brief moment, in the enriching and less technology-dependent realms of dance, drama, music, literature, and visual arts.

In this collection, I offer you a series of my literary retreats spanning two years. Some stories flowed effortlessly, as if born from a dream, while others demanded a battle against the allure of settling for mediocrity versus striving for originality and depth. There were also instances where I had to resist the urge to procrastinate and avoid succumbing to complete social isolation as I toiled away at my craft.

I am deeply grateful for the support and encouragement of friends and fellow creatives who challenged me to improve while tethering me to the realities of life. Special recognition is owed to Anthony Seda for his dual role in this regard, as well as to my companions at Bel Air Creative Writers Society: Robert Broomall, Alan Amrhine, Terry Emery, Keith Hoskins, and Lisa Janele. Additionally, I extend my gratitude to Indies United Publishing House for providing a nurturing home for my work.

To you, dear reader, I sincerely hope this collection has brought you enjoyment and has lived up to the expectations set forth on the back cover.

Thanks for Reading!

If you like *The Unwanted Guest and other short thrillers*, please consider leaving a review! Indie and small press authors can't survive without word-of-mouth referrals from readers like you.

About the Author

TIM grew up in Syracuse, New York. He currently resides in Maryland where he teaches English, Creative Writing, and Journalism on the High School Level. At the insistence of his former middle school students, he began writing seriously in 2014.

He credits his love for story to his mother, who spent countless hours reading to him and his siblings when they were growing up. Growing up, he devoured the literary words of C. S. Lewis, J. R. R. Tolkien, Piers Anthony, and many others. Mysteries, thrillers, and fantasies are among the genre he most frequently reads.

When he's not writing, he's reading, teaching, enjoying a live music concert, smoking cigars, or shooting lead down range at speeds of two thousand feet per second.

Visit Tim on the Web

www.timothyrbaldwin.com
facebook.com/timothyrbaldwin
instagram.com/timothyrbaldwin

Don't miss out!

Visit the website below and you can sign up to receive emails whenever Timothy R. Baldwin publishes a new book. There's no charge and no obligation.

https://books2read.com/r/B-A-PUHJ-RVZWC

BOOKS 2 READ

Connecting independent readers to independent writers.

INDIES UNITED PUBLISHING HOUSE, LLC

About the Publisher

Here at Indies United, we are a co-op of like-minded authors working together to showcase our books, and our diversity as writers, that embrace over a dozen different genres. We openly encourage and support both new and established authors in their pursuit of finding their audience while bringing to you books worth reading.

To find out more, visit us at: https://www.indiesunited.net/